THE THIRD TEMPTATION

ALSO BY DENIS WILLIAMS

Other Leopards (1963, 2009)
Giglioli in Guyana 1922–1972 (1972)
Image and Idea in the Arts of Guyana (1970)
Icon and Image: A Study of Sacred and Secular Forms of African
  Classical Art (1974)
Contemporary Art in Guyana (1976)
Guyana, Colonial Art to Revolutionary Art (1976)
Ancient Guyana (1985)
Pages in Guyanese Prehistory (1995)
Prehistoric Guiana (2004)

THE THIRD TEMPTATION

DENIS WILLIAMS

INTRODUCTION BY VICTOR J. RAMRAJ

PEEPAL TREE

First published in Great Britain in 1968
by Calder and Boyars
This new edition published in 2010
Peepal Tree Press Ltd
17 King's Avenue
Leeds LS6 1QS
England

ISBN13: 978 1 84523 068 5

Supported by
ARTS COUNCIL
ENGLAND

INTRODUCTION

VICTOR J. RAMRAJ

The Third Temptation (1968) is the second of Denis Williams's two novels – the first was *Other Leopards* (1963) – and it appears very different in thematic and formal preoccupations. *Other Leopards*, set in Johkara (a fictional version of the Sudan), explores the search for identity of a self-divided West Indian in an imperial-colonial context complicated by racial, cultural, and historical particulars. The protagonists and most of the secondary characters divide between those from the formerly colonising powers and those from the developing world. *The Third Temptation*, set in Caedmon, a seaside resort in north Wales in the United Kingdom, concentrates on moral and spiritual issues in the context not of colonial politics but of sensuality, passion, and betrayal. The players, whether residents or visitors, are all Europeans. The differences in form are even starker: in *Other Leopards*, though there are occasional instances of stylistic experimentation with poetic and stream-of-consciousness prose, the form is that of the conventional novel. *The Third Temptation* is highly experimental. Williams (who was as much a painter and anthropologist as a writer), impatient with the inability of the novel form to capture simultaneity (as the cinema or painting can do) and frustrated with this constrictive linearity, turns with a sense of liberation to multiple time sequences, multiple points of view, and multiple, fast-changing loci, presented with no immediately obvious cohesion, no apparently integrating connections. The result is a work of fiction that challenges and may at times exasperate. But *The Third Temptation*, though it does not have the easy accessibility and the explicit postcolonial appeal of *Other Leopards*, is a work that rewards perseverance, deserving of recognition as a formidable achievement and one of the Caribbean's relatively small number of accomplished avant-garde novels.

What initially appears to be the central incident in the three hours of a summer morning that frames the time sequence of the novel – the death of a young man in a traffic accident on Sweeley Street in the business district of Caedmon – turns out to be insignificant in itself. The young man remains unnamed and is barely portrayed. This accident is the means by which Williams introduces three contiguous relationships of unrequited and unfulfilled love. The central relationship – a love triangle – involves Joss (Joshua) Banks, the retired owner of a printing works, Banks Press; Laurence Henry Owens (known by his initialism, Lho), a commercial artist, one of Joss's former staff; and Lho's wife, Bid. We learn that just under three years before the present of the novel, Joss has seduced Bid and when Lho discovers that the child she is bearing is not his, he hangs himself in woods close to Caedmon. Joss subsequently marries Bid, though on the day of the traffic accident they are estranged. Joss is in fact on his way to his former business on a mission to recover some of Lho's artwork in an attempt to please Bid. On the basis of this and some previous visits, Joss's former colleagues comment that he is "going to seed" (p. 73; all page references are to this edition). There are hints that he may feel guilty about the role he has played in Lho's demise.

The second narrative involves Sean, a young man who, at the time of the traffic accident, is chatting with Joss about his girlfriend who has left him. Sean shows Joss a letter that he plans to send to her in which he threatens to kill himself – a situation that is evidently intended as a parallel to Lho's suicide. We learn that Joss had once attempted to seduce Sean's girlfriend and he now advises Sean to leave her, mocking the suicide threat and cynically telling him that all he needs is an obligation-free, occasional sexual diversion. But Sean insists that though she is "a liar, thief, tramp" (p. 121), he loves her. At the end of the novel, Sean is desperately looking for the letter which, on Joss's advice, he has crumpled up and thrown away. Joss's mockery of the suicide threat is notably hypocritical and even more unsympathetic than it seems, since he is later to confess (but not to Sean) that he once nearly killed himself because of an unhappy relationship.

The third narrative involves Joss again. At some point during the three hours of the novel, he meets an attractive woman, Chloë – whom he refers to, in conversation with Sean, as "the blonde bitch" – in St. John's Church. Chloë, "the Chronicle Girl" (p. 95), is visiting Caedmon on behalf of her newspaper in a "Lobby Lud" promotion.[1] They compare experiences with their respective spouses and other sexual partners, revealing much of themselves in a compulsive Ancient-Mariner manner. They appear to be attracted to each other, but after Joss's initial attempt to seduce Chloë he is reluctant to give in to her overtures, claiming loss of passion with age. However, Joss may have something else on his mind. His attempt to persuade Titch, his former number two, now the manager of the printworks, to return Lho's artwork has been unsuccessful. Titch refuses, provokes Joss with a jibe about bad conscience, and is pushed by a furious Joss into a vat in the foundry where lead for type is being melted down. Titch is evidently seriously injured, though not yet dead. These three narratives outlined here have to be pieced together as in a jigsaw puzzle.

Through his portrayal of Joss, Williams explores the nature of power and the powerful – his central concern in this novel. In *Other Leopards*, it is political power that holds his attention. The Afro-Guyanese protagonist, Lionel/Lobo Froad, is up against his British boss, Hughie, who, he feels, humiliates him, and from whom he attempts to emancipate himself by what may or may not be a successful attempt to murder him. The power play at work in *The Third Temptation* has to do with power among individuals in the rush and stress of everyday lives.

Joss, as the former owner of the town's newspaper, *The Cambrian Weekly*, has dominated his staff and friends, intruding on their personal and private lives. This naked use of power has been challenged only by Lho, and it is he who introduces into the narrative the motif of the three temptations of Christ, to which the novel's title refers. Praying in the Garden of Gethsemane, Christ is tempted by Satan with the offer of power over the kingdoms of the world should Christ worship him. Christ rejects this third temptation as he does the earlier temptations – the first to make bread to satiate his hunger, the second to perform a great stunt by spectacularly throwing himself off a mountain and being saved by angels.[2] Though Joss very explicitly rejects Lho's interpretation of this biblical episode, it has clearly found its way into his consciousness. Lho sees satisfying hunger and giving in to vanity as venial, but not the desire for power over others which he sees as irrevocably linked with evil:

> "Power? Whence is it offered or conferred? Who is the agent? – a concept different from the other two, terrible in *divine* implication; a true temptation, profoundly horrifying…. So he clobbered to the inescapable conclusion that power and evil are one – and divine. Yet he abjured it, feared it wherever he found it… in anyone" (p. 62; emphasis added).

But if Lho thinks that power and evil are inextricably linked, and that both are divinely inspired (which perhaps accounts for his suicide), the novel as a whole suggests a more differentiated reading of the nature of power. In its structure, the novel brings together the fatal Sweeley Street accident and the circumstances leading to Lho's suicide. This accident, as observed by the protagonists and numerous other characters with just walk-on or incidental roles, is seen variously as pure chance (a "blue Ford swung out at a lick from the curve; the youth in the red Mini-van didn't stand a chance in hell" (p. 75)) or as fated by divine power and intended as a lesson by the Almighty. The character who is possibly a revenant Lho seems to be implying this when he says, "No one is chastened by the tragedy; it will happen again" (p. 58). Joss's use of power on the other hand is unambiguously evil, resulting in Lho's suicide, the attempted murder of Titch, and in his involvement in what may or may not have been a hit-and-run death of a boy in the immediate past (Joss's story is of a boy who was bird-nesting and had fallen into the path of his car on the road). A minor character (though Williams might disagree with the use of the word "minor" – presenting all points of view as important) sees Joss as the "spitting image" of the painting of Christ in St. John's Church. The text is not suggesting that Joss is Christ-like; on the contrary, the comparison sets up a contrast between Christ's refusal to give in to the third temptation and Joss's acquiescence to it.

This emphasis on spiritual issues is new in Williams's work. *Other Leopards* does touch on the conflict between Muslims and Christians, but it is not given any spiritual-doctrinal underpinning, and is seen mainly as an added aggravation to intra-regional political conflicts. At around the same time as he was writing *The Third Temptation*, Williams was also exhibiting a fascination with the Christ figure in his art work. While living in the Mazaruni area of Guyana, after his return there from the UK in 1968, he painted what he considered one of his finest paintings, *The Majesta*, a portrait of Christ, using leaves reflecting various degrees of light for his face.

The moral and spiritual centre of the novel comes in the dramatic meeting of Joss and Chloë in the church, where – though the novel refuses commentary or explanations – Joss's revelations can be read as clues as to how Williams sees the psychological motivations – of one man at least – to exercising power abusively. It is a motivation, Joss's confessions suggest, rooted, paradoxically, in his hidden self-perceptions of powerlessness.

In the church, Chloë finds Joss trembling violently, apparently in prayer, and refusing to look at her (though he has seen her earlier in the street). He pours out to her his sense of rottenness and confesses to various shaming episodes in his past (though nothing about his assault on Titch). It is in their dialogue that we appear to get an indication of Joss's spiritual desolation. With respect to his confessions, Joss tells her, "You've done better in a few minutes than all the people I've ever known put together" (p. 103). Given that we are never offered any confirmation of the truth or falsity of any of the character's statements, and given that Joss has also just propositioned Chloë, we have to wonder how serious Joss is when he makes this comment. The fact, though, that Joss backs off from the "seduction" (it is fact Chloë who makes the move, interrupted only when the painting of the allegedly eye-opening Jesus clatters to the floor) does suggest that it is safe to read the statement as signalling Joss's vulnerability rather than any quality in Chloë as a listener. Where this leads to in the trajectory of Joss's life Williams leaves open, but it is clear that Joss is no longer the man he once was, though it is also evident that the sources of his distress extend far back into his childhood. He has a Calvinist sense of existing in a divinely ordained world ("so it is ordained" is a repeated phrase), but one in which the odds are stacked up against him as a victim. In confessional mode he tells Chloë about a terrible childhood dream in which a boy is condemned to eat a granite mountain outside his bedroom window before daybreak, and is terrified of the morning not just because of the task, but "because he might meet the person who set him the task and then he would have to destroy this person…" (p. 97). There are his confessions of shooting one of his platoon during the war, a man too frightened to expose himself to enemy fire, and of shooting a mortally wounded enemy combatant. Too truly, as he confesses to Chlöe, "there's blood on my hands all right" (p. 99), but what is significant in all these stories (and that of the boy who allegedly falls in the path of his car from a bird-nesting accident) is Joss's sense of outrage that these things should happen to him. He shoots the man not to put him out of his misery but *because he made it happen to me*" (p. 119, emphasis in original). What is evident in his confessions (to a stranger he is unlikely to see again) is that he does not take responsibility for his actions or seek forgiveness. Defiantly he blames the "murderees" for their plight: "I nearly stepped on a mass of pulp with a head on it begging me to put it out of its miseries" (p. 119). For Joss his actions seem to be simply matters of justifiable self-preservation. To Chloë he denies that it is a sin: "it's mortal power, if you like but no sin" (p. 102), but it seems evident that Lho's words are eating away in his consciousness.

After his extraordinary exchange with Chloë, Joss meets up with Sean in a pub, and in a state of agitation tries to keep Sean with him, for the company. Joss admits he is "feeling sort of sick" but blames Sean's "boiled shrimps", not his agitated frame of mind (p. 118). He tells Sean that he just met "the Chronicle bitch; lovely bit of skin" but not that he has confessed so much to her. Sean himself is concerned only with recovering his letter. The letter – in two forms, as a draft on a torn-up seaside postcard and as a fair copy on what is now a screwed up piece of paper – has several functions in the novel: as a connecting device (both letter and card pass through a number of hands) and as a counter-statement to the poisonous misogyny of both Joss's talk and behaviour. Sean's letter is an admission of male vulnerability and need for completion in relationship with a woman. Between Joss's bleak vision of kill or be killed, and Lho's advocacy of responsibility and resistance to the temptations of power lies the novel's moral centre, dramatised but in no sense resolved.

In comparison with *Other Leopards*, as has already been suggested, the exploration of power in this novel appears detached from the issues of colonialism and race. If, for instance, Denis Williams is pointing to the emergence of power-hungry politicians in the Caribbean at the time he was writing this novel – Eric Williams in Trinidad or Forbes Burnham in Guyana – he does so obliquely. However, closer reading shows that the absence of the colonial and postcolonial world is by no means complete. The novel touches on the colonial-like status of Wales in contrast to the dominant Englishness represented by Joss (a "foreigner" from Birmingham). It underscores the colonised Welshness of Lho and Bid, subordinated in unsuccessful opposition to Banks's colonising Englishness, when we learn that "Bid had all but lost her language in long and alien communication with Joss", and that when the maritally betrayed Lho goes to a remote hut to paint, he also goes to repair his Welshness and becomes so very Welsh as to be "incomprehensible consequently to his countrymen" (p. 66). This sounds like an echo of Lionel's impossible quest to recover African Lobo; and in the relationship between Joss and Lho there are echoes of Hughie and Lionel in *Other Leopards*, since Lho seriously contemplates killing Joss, before actually killing himself.

There are, too, recurring references to a bronze statue given to Caedmon by an appreciative, unnamed African country. It is of a celebrated Welsh missionary "who martyred himself for the planting of Christianity in Darkest Africa" (p. 43). The novel ends with this statue: "At the foot of the bronze statue the island now lies bare in the sun" (p. 134). The statue is a prominent landmark in Caedmon and its recurrence in the novel is primarily as an indicator of the multiple geographic points of view Williams employs in his ambitious undertaking of capturing the totality of the location. But the incidental details provided about the statue suggest a consciousness of colonial politics that cannot be wholly suppressed from the novel. The fictional statue could very likely be that of William Hughes, an actual missionary to the Congo, who, forced by illness to return to Wales, founded Colwyn Bay's Congo Missionary Training Institute, which ran between 1891 and 1911, to provide biblical instruction and missionary training for Africans who returned to their homes as evangelists.[3] The Williams of *Other Leopards* most likely would have pounced on this historical incident for its rich narrative possibilities, but the Williams of *The Third Temptation* evidently considers it out of place in this novel, though he could not omit it altogether. The presence of the statue hints at the kind of imperial resonance that a later writer of Guyanese origins, David Dabydeen, explores in his novel, *Our Lady of Demerara* (2004), in the connection created between the life of an old priest in Coventry in England, who has once been a missionary in British Guiana, and the expedition the novel's white English protagonist makes to the hinterland of Guyana.

There are other biographical contexts for the novel that Williams seems to quite consciously ignore. He lived with his family in North Wales for a while and was evidently aware of the racial problems his daughter, Charlotte Williams, experienced growing up in Llandudno, which she records in her memoir *Sugar and Slate* (2002). (The "sugar" in the title is her father's Afro-Caribbean heritage; the "slate" is her mother's Welshness.) Williams captures the landscape and language of North Wales but not his daughter's question of whether "to be mixed was not to be mixed up, or was it?" (*Sugar and Slate*, p.), and her awareness of an undeniable feeling of difference, and of having to contend with their neighbours' incomprehension, curiosity, and painful awkwardness in relating to her family. Williams does, though, introduce the mixed marriage of the blonde Chloë to a black man (in the shorthand of stereotypes of 1950's Britain, Williams hints that he may be a West Indian – he presents himself in bed in his British Rail uniform) in her discussion with Joss in the church, when she tells him that their lovemaking involved dirty, racial love-talk:

"he could only get going by calling me white swine and trash... and I'd say to him 'Come on me black baboon...'" (p. 105). Other than this striking instance – which is never taken further – race is ignored in this novel. In *Other Leopards*, race compounds the Afro-Guyanese protagonist's relationship with his English boss's Welsh secretary, Catherine, who at one point asks him, "You ever wish you were white...?" (Williams, 2009, p. 42) *The Third Temptation* relegates race to the background while foregrounding the exploration of what Williams seems to be saying is more fundamental than race or culture: the third temptation to power. Chloë's briefly mentioned relationship with her black husband serves as yet another illustration of the power-play between individuals that leads to regret and recrimination. In *Other Leopards*, there is a strong sense of the worlds that constitute Lionel Froad's divided psyche, conveyed in the portraits of the two female protagonists vying for his attention: Eve of Guyana is seen in terms of gloomy forest floors and dark, silent rivers, while Catherine of Wales is likened to "those distilled, shadowless twilights you get at times in the Welsh valleys, illumined from the clouds" (Williams, 2009, p. 78). In *The Third Temptation*, though there is an offhand reference to "the virgin forests of Guyana" (p. 28), when Joss looks at a small globe in his office, little is made of this elsewhere in the novel. But it is hard not to think of Caribbean history when Williams introduces the recurrent saying (credited to Titch, who is from Poland and may have the Nazis in mind) that: "There are two kinds of men, those with whips and those with wounds. There are no other..." (p. 99). Joss repeats this on several occasions and while it is offered as a universal truth by him, the subtext of Caribbean resonance is hard to ignore.

If *The Third Temptation* is marked by an apparent avoidance of explicit postcolonial issues, what is immediately striking is its impressive experimentation with form, and in this at least is its greatest pertinence to the postcolonial Caribbean novel. Such experimentation is not unknown in West Indian writing. As early as 1926, Eric Walrond's *Tropic Death*, in disdaining traditional unity and coherence, has to be seen as one of the early texts that ushered in the modernist form. Edgar Mittelholzer's *A Morning at the Office* (1950) explores multiple points of view within a three-hour unity of time and place, as well as the connective role of physical motifs, and his *Latticed Echoes* (1960) tries out the leitmotif form, with setting given on one page and action and dialogue on the facing page. Wilson Harris's celebrated *Palace of the Peacock* (1960) and most of his later novels have eschewed realist form, adopting what could be seen on one level as an early instance of magic realism. More recently, Fred D'Aguiar employs various realist and non-realist techniques to access the interiority of a troubled child in *Bethany/Bettany* (2003). As already noted, Williams eschews the linearity of nineteenth-century narrative and, in what approximates magic realism, he has a man "whose face in the slanting sunlight seems lilac, of a chalky texture" (p. 32), who appears to be the dead Lho, walking among the living in the current time sequence of the novel. Williams, indeed, begins the novel with Lho's thoughts on the verge of or soon after his suicide, ransacking the worlds of diction, imagery, and rhythm for the right evocation of such a mind: "It seemed that he was spinning in this void, that it was radiant, spinning; that the endless instant was shrieking with a vertiginous mad sourcelessness…" (p. 24).

What is especially marked in *The Third Temptation* is the novel's self-reflexiveness about its treatment of point of view, both visual and psychological. This metafictional thread draws our attention to Williams's belief in the limitations of conventional narrative in capturing the truth about human individuals, about what actually goes on in an individual's mind. Numerous comments are made that allude to experimental techniques in the form of the novel by various characters and by the elusive narrator (whose voice is evident, though it is sometimes hard to pinpoint when exactly he is speaking, or whether we are hearing Lho). With its rapid shifts in point of view, and Williams's refusal to use the conventions that distinguish between voices, there is a deliberate maintenance of uncertainty. Even so, there are enough clues for a careful reader to make intelligent guesses. We know that it is Joss, for instance, who asserts that "I don't want to read another story ever; what's the use; the most remarkable stories remain locked up inside each man impossible of telling – no one would dare" (p. 50).

Seeming to believe that there is no reality outside human consciousness, Williams gives multiple points of view of particular settings and events in time, often within minutes of each other. So there are numerous repetitions of a scene or incident, with only slight variations. Phrases are repeated: "the man with the lilac face" (p. 83), "The blue paper ball" (p. 53, 109), "The pregnant woman in the pink smock" (p. 28, 31, 32), "the man in the blue anorak" (p. 17). The narrative alerts us to the slight but incremental variations in the portraits and thus to the shifting nature of reality: "At various distances the pregnant woman therefore wears a pink smock, a pink and white, or a mauve, depending on the locus of observation" (p. 32). Williams hints at his reason for offering different snapshots in time: "Time, withdrawn from activity, discloses motion suspended – intention, promise – as in a snapshot, as on a Grecian urn…" (p. 107). However, unlike Keats, Williams does not appear to see "motion suspended" as offering any kind of solace from ephemerality and mortality, but as a falsification of the flux of life in time. Hence the explicit struggle to be precise about the temporal and spatial location of events – barring accurate content "there is no meaning" (p. 107). Nevertheless, the novel acknowledges the necessary compromise that the author must select details for readers, as "it is difficult to rein the attention; beckoned hither and thither it is embarrassed by the multiplicity of the data and their conflicting claims, perceptual and emotional… beyond a certain plane a selective perceptiveness is required" (p. 93). But the selectivity must not be too restrictive, a rubric that Williams adheres to in this novel. A cursory look at the opening of the chapter (or time slot) entitled "11.15 – 12 Noon" illustrates the multiplicities that inform the style. The first section appears to be the narrator's voice giving us a panoramic picture of Caedmon beach. But it could just as well be the voice of Joss Banks or even Lho, either of whom could be looking at a postcard with a beach scene painted by a minor Fauvist that dissolves into the Caedmon beach scene. The next section begins with this puzzling sentence: "To the face-worn image distorted now at the sagging end and chapter's close in the universe of the copperpipe he might be uttering an ancestral No!" (p. 115). It requires reading to the end of the entire section to realise that this is a description of Joss Banks, standing at a urinal, contemplating his aging face reflected in a copper pipe.

Focusing strictly on what happens during the slice of time up to midday, Williams leaves many situations unresolved, unconcluded. We do not know whether Sean will be reconciled with his girlfriend. We do not know whether Titch is in fact dead or horribly disfigured, or whether Tom, Titch's colleague, will air his suspicion that Joss is responsible for what has happened to Titch, or if Joss has again exercised his bullying power on Tom, who begins by hinting his suspicions, but ends by smoothing things over and offering Joss the art work (pp. 125-129). We *do* know that many think that Joss is disintegrating physically and perhaps emotionally. But is his presence in St John's Church evidence of remorse? In the church, he embarks on a confession to Chloë that omits Titch, but opens himself up in way that he has probably never done before. Yet we also see that he is ready to desecrate the church, to have sex with Chloë in the pews. Is his later visit to the pub indicative of his being a troubled man? But Williams proceeds no further with plots or subplots beyond "12 Noon" – the heading of the last section of the novel.

In his experiments with point of view, Williams employs a modified version of the *je-néant* or the "absent I", practised by Alain Robbe-Grillet and members of the *Nouveau Roman* School in the 1950s. Joss perceives himself both in the first and third person, shifting from one to the other arbitrarily. Certain individuals and incidents are returned to and presented in mixed, altered ways, depending on the loci and the consciousness employed. Williams heightens these multiple viewpoints through the pervasive presence of mirrors and reflections – alerting us to how, as a painter-novelist, he places great emphasis on physical setting. He draws attention to angles and framing (echoing Robbe-Grillet's complementary cinematic techniques), and to colours, hues, shadows, shapes, sizes, perspectives, depth and the focal distance of particular scenes. Lho the artist is, appropriately, the source of many of these reflections in the novel. It is perhaps worth noting that Williams takes experimentation in the Caribbean novel to a very different place than Harris. If Harris writes a fiction of spiritual allegory in which physical image leads metaphorically to transcendental vision, Williams's experiment is altogether more Joycean in having a super-realist focus on the plurality of the physical image as a means towards representing the world of human affairs.

The painter in Williams is clearly attracted to Robbe-Grillet's theory of writing about "pure surface". For writers of the *Nouveau Roman* school, outward and intensive descriptions of objects replace or complement psychological or inner depiction of character. They expect readers to piece together the story and determine the emotional resonance of a scene without apparent authorial direction. Anticipating the postmoderns, they undermine the possibility of any single given meaning, theorising that their novels ultimately can mean many things to many different readers. But Williams is a modernist rather than a postmodernist. Though he employs fragmentation and collage (to reflect a fragmented world), he still appears to believe that there is a truth out there that can be accessed. He still seems to believe in cause-and-effect, even though there is no overt sequential narrative or conventional character development. But perhaps, if we accept Robbe-Grillet's theory of multiple meanings, it may be that Williams, at least in *The Third Temptation*, sees no truth or order outside human consciousness.

Whether he succeeds in creating a wholly realised subversion of the traditional novel form, readers must decide for themselves. In Caribbean critical discourse *The Third Temptation* has been overshadowed by *Other Leopards*, perhaps because of its challenging experimental, avant-garde form and its preoccupation with philosophical-spiritual matters rather than with overtly postcolonial issues, though its focus on the temptations of power is all too prescient with respect to postcolonial politics. As it is set in Wales and peopled by English and Welsh characters, it is, unfortunately, sometimes considered as not properly a Caribbean novel. In this respect it may be compared to V. S. Naipaul's *Mr Stone and the Knights Companion*, set exclusively in London with white British protagonists. And just as Naipaul may reveal himself most fully as a Trinidadian Indian who is imaginatively exploring his Caribbean Hindu heritage in this apparently "English" novel, so perhaps we should also see *The Third Temptation* as far more rooted in Caribbean concerns than it at first appears. In its experimentation with form it challenges all simplifications of the Caribbean's complex reality. It effectively alerts us to both the virtues and limitations of writing in comparison to visual forms of representation; it questions those assumptions that seek to corral the Caribbean writer within any narrowly defined focus of legitimate concerns; and it prompts the reader to see, beyond and through given historical forms of oppression, that the temptations of power have no limitations of race, culture or time. It is undoubtedly a challenging work, but persevered with and read attentively, a rewarding and stimulating one – even if we read it only as a ludic work, for as Williams says of the pageant of imagery in the novel, it can be "a game and nothing more" (p. 107).

Notes

1. A "Lobby Lud" is a newspaper employee who anonymously visits seaside resorts to drum up circulation among people on vacation. The newspaper publishes details of the particular town where it has assigned that day's "Lobby Lud". A pass phrase is also published. Anyone carrying a copy of the newspaper could accost the Lobby Lud with the appropriate phrase and receive a sum of money. Incidentally, Sean asks Joss if Chloë is a £100 or £500 Lobby Lud (p. 120). Williams may have known that in *Brighton Rock* (1938), Graham Greene employs a Lobby Lud character, Kolley Kibber. The Lobby Lud was first used by a UK newspaper, the *Westminster Gazette*, in 1927.

2. This is the order of the temptations as given by Matthew, Chapter 4. However, Luke, Chapter 4, inverts the second and third. Biblical commentators believe that Matthew adheres to the true chronological order while Luke's order is topical. Biblical commentators wonder about the nature of power that Satan offers Christ, most accepting that it is not so much political power with which Christ is tempted, but more the power to influence people with his message.

3. Martin M'Caw, a researcher at Bristol University, has noted that Hughes was an early advocate of Africans worshipping in their own

language, which set him against the missionary establishment. The West Africans, however, "appreciated his support for their freedom of cultural expression". M'Caw contends that "his influence was far-reaching – the local missionaries trained by Hughes might well have been an influence on the postcolonial generation including independence prime ministers such as Jomo Kenyatta (Kenya), Hastings Banda (Malawi) and Kwame Nkrumah of Ghana" (M'Caw, 2008, p. 6).

Works Cited

Dabydeen, David. *Our Lady of Demerara*. Chichester: Dido Press, 2004; Leeds: Peepal Tree Press, 2009.

D'Aguiar, Fred. *Bethany/Bettany*. London: Chatto and Windus, 2003.

Greene, Graham. *Brighton Rock*. London: Heinemann, 1938.

Harris, Wilson. *Palace of the Peacock*. London: Faber, 1960.

M'Caw, Martin. Research Paper presented at Bangor University on "William Hughes, Baptist Minister", 21 Oct. 2008. [Reported in *The Baptist Times*, Oct. 2008: 6].

Mittelholzer, Edgar. *A Morning at the Office*. London: Hogarth Press, 1950; London: Heinemann, 1974; Leeds: Peepal Tree Press, 2009.
——. *Latticed Echoes*. London: Secker and Warburg, 1960.

Naipaul, V.S. *Mr Stone and the Knights Companion*. London: Andre Deutsch, 1963.

Ramraj, Victor J. "Denis Williams". *Fifty Caribbean Writers*. Ed Daryl Dance. New York: Greenwood, 1986. 483-92.

Robbe-Grillet, Alain. *For a New Novel [Pour un Nouveau Roman]*. 1963. New York: Grove Press, 1965.
——. *The Erasers [Les Gommes]*. 1963. New York: Grove Press, 1973.

Walrond, Eric. *Tropic Death*. 1926. New York: Macmillan-Collier, 1972.

Williams, Charlotte. *Sugar and Slate*. London: Planet, 2002.

Williams, Denis. *Other Leopards*. London: New Authors, 1963; and Leeds: Peepal Tree Press [Caribbean Modern Classics], 2009.

Victor J. Ramraj, University of Calgary

For Miles

midnight

He had been aware of a voice – it seemed a voice, there and not there, wavering, now near, now far, like a quality of the darkness – a circumambience that might possess being but no centre, a function of space and yet not space, as sound is a function of the drum and yet not the drum. He could see nothing, naturally, but knew himself suspended somewhere, at some great height, above the incomprehensible tumult perhaps, breathing darkness.

An interval ago there had been the sense that he had drowned – the wavering had achieved a vibration which it was not easy to tell whether he had been hearing, no, or merely feeling; it existed all around and through him. It could have been that he was himself the source and author of this sound, its locus and centre, that with his end it too would end. Then he had stopped knowing, feeling; nothingness had supervened, for the duration of which he had lost even the sense of immaterial suspension. It was an interval merely. Now looking back he saw that he had not drowned; though continuing to perish his body was surely alive, maybe kicking. Without effort he could distinguish this previous state from the suspended nothingness which dwelled in him, there and not there, rippling with the sound of subterranean water, the pebbly sound of raindrops, ashen, rasping, horripilating, the rasp, sodden air, dead leaves dead in his nostrils, swelling retreating, so that in the still darkness its prowling roar seemed to disclose measures of an unseen and terrible space whose quivering cavities relayed echoes to further terribly trembling spaces there and not there.

By these means he knew that he lingered after all in some finite space; that the end though surely close was yet to come. But the feeling of suspension, of distance from the tumult, persisted. It seemed to him that he was by turns centre or edge or limit of this migrant space, cold, but finite. And now that he wished to re-enter the tumult this space bellied around him like the curve of sky. In darkness limited by threshold sound he was this space, pregnant now it seemed too with a quality of light, a brilliance. He strained after a measure with which to comprehend this space, this darkness, but in face of the radiance the register faded to insignificance. He could not use his mind; he had lost that power.

He felt afraid, an apprehension which he had not before the interval or immediately after it felt. A fear of what, or whom – and why? In vain he tried to get back, but irreversibly this power was now denied him. Then he knew that he was going to die. By means of the void around and through him he tried to utter this into the darkness that was left of himself. But his tongue had filled his mouth, already dead.

It seemed that he was spinning in this void, that it was radiant, spinning; that the endless instant was shrieking with a vertiginous mad sourcelessness:

A legend, Lho, even though apt, is truth only from a certain plane.

He could no longer answer; he had taken the world with him, uncomprehending.

As though stricken in urgent utterance the lips were parted. Beneath the cooing of wood-pigeons the bell-like chant: a sequence of notes, first three, then two, that barely echoed in the memory before, from a different position but always solicitously close, the chant went up again. Caught on an invisible thread a withered leaf turned. Turned and turned, languorous. A shower of others held the dew like stars in his damp hair and on his shoulders or floated in the gloom. The woods rattled with the pebbly sound of raindrops falling on the sodden carpet underfoot. Beneath a halo of fresh glistening cobweb Lho, alternately centre or edge or limit of this sound, hung in a dreadful stillness. Solemn as eternity the ash thrust its crown into the forest roof. Gravity, inertia, the conjoined sheets taut between cruel stresses; for typically Lho had inserted the nether end to a vagrant root some distance off – an elaboration as characteristic as it was subtle – and interposed a single coil around the branch between his weight and the point of greatest strain. The logic implicit in the final image would, I think, have pleased him. I grab the dangling body; it swings towards me, kicking, remote to the end. I shriek:

A man may perceive the error of God and yet not budge, Lho, it's so easy to father a legend!

As slowly the corpse pivots.

Then the constable is on his island jewelled in the morning sun.

The constable is not on his island, but on the pavement walking – heavy, from the hips, bent forward, looking down. I follow him. I tear Sean's postcard up and throw it into the waste-bin outside Marks and Spencers. It drops in four equal fragments. There is already a banana peel there and Sean's balled-up blue notepaper. Then the constable is on his island, jewelled, as though he'd never left it. Sean's balled-up blue notepaper is in my hand as I cross the zebra, cross the pregnant woman crossing the zebra, whose back appears in the show window of the butcher's with the distance opening between us. And there is the constable mopping his brow. Though the sun has suddenly gone and the light is grey-green now the constable mops his brow and pivots towards Trwyn Mawr, looking up the hill. And then he leans over, listening to the pregnant woman, and together they look in my direction. I gain the pavement observing them in the butcher's window, wondering, but not for long, since the constable merely grins and the woman waddles on. And is the constable looking up the hill?

The constable is looking towards the hill, beyond the round-about, at nothing in particular.

And the man in the Mini-van – is he dead?

It is thought that the man in the Mini-van died on the spot. Some time will elapse though, before the wreckage is cleared. The man in the Mini-van did not die on the spot. Titch, returning, says so. It is known that the fragments of flesh were twitching still, convulsively, as he was borne into the ambulance. Though it is certain that he must be dead by now he is not known to be dead. It is known however that the van bore a Conway trade name.

It cannot be said that the constable ever looks at nothing in particular; he has been trained out of that. The constable looks always definitely at something: at objects or persons, sometimes discrete, more often in association. He is the centre of a visual field, an aural frame in which, close at hand, a red Mini-van slips into the traffic stream at the roundabout behind a cycling club – yellow stripes and black pedalling down the hill – trafficator flashing, flashing yet as the constable waves the van down at the zebra before the youth in the khaki smock behind the wheel could achieve a satisfactory acceleration, gritting his teeth as on a bit. Their eyes connect like buffers in the railway yard. The crowd spills onto the zebra, interweaving. In the foreground of the aural frame the sound of footsteps is like hailstones on zinc, louder than the soughing of voices which, in turn, fills a wider aural frame. In the Mini-van the eyes of the youth remain on those of the constable, impatient, protesting, who though is looking towards the hill, into the bronze eyes of the statue placed there by an African government, weathered, bleached on brows, cheeks, shoulders, its protuberances etched like highlights against the grey rockface, against the patina of the figure itself. The doors of the van are open; it is stacked to the roof. Only one door of the van is open: the left rear door:

Banks Pr

Job Prin

Photo En

Commerci

The Camb

Somebody exclaims: O gay, taa!

Titch is not in the press room.

Then the van starts up and moves away.

Lho's old designs, remember them – the ones he did of Bid – remember?

Tom remembers, doesn't remember, goes silent, embarrassed. Then asks: Seen Titch about them, then?

Titch's out!

Titch's there; down in the press room. He's there.

Tom's playing the bloody goat, the bloody bleating goat. Why should you listen to the bleat of a bloody goat Joss Banks, Job Printer, Photo Engraver, Commercial Designer, Editor?

Because you've had it, Joss. Titch's rolling in the lolly now; Tom's running the *Record* – that's why.

My old swivel-chair, *my* old wallpaper blooming with damp, *my* old office globe, dusty, Victorian amber, soft on the eyes, where the world is three foot high, the whole room compacted – the windows, desk, me, the floor, ceiling – in the globe's convexity. How masterful to rotate the earth with one's fingertips – 50° …60°…longitude east…80°…90°…100° to Gilbert Island 180°; then back to 170°…160°…130° longitude west…120°…110°… 100°, Galapagos Islands 60°…the Amazon 40°…Equator…Torrid zone…Alto Trombetas…the virgin forests of Guyana…

What I mean. Nobody's using them or anything, I need them Tom, they're – you know – private like.

Sure, Joss, sure. Hang on a moment, Titch'll be up in half a mo', half a mo' he'll be.

He's dead!

No, Titch returning says he did not die; it is thought that he might be twitching in anguish even now – the spasmic twitch of life released from will.

But is he dead, then?

This is what the pregnant woman in the pink smock, beneath the shoulder of the constable on the island, wants to know. The incident is bad for her, she can be heard to say; she would not like to tell her husband.

Where though, is the husband of the pregnant woman?

The husband of the pregnant woman has told her to await him near the roundabout, on the roundabout, on one of the concave benches below the flower boxes, from which she could look at the traffic, the crowd, that statue of the great Welsh martyr which has been presented – so the inscription reads – by an African government to the people of Caedmon. Imperceptibly a red Mini-van approaches the zebra, people swirling about it back and front. Visible through the window a pair of hands, the cuffs of a khaki smock, a raw young profile covered with pimples. The hair and back of the head are cut off by the body of the van above which is the Woolworths sign, gold on a red ground, shades darker than the colour of the van which, incredibly, is still crawling towards the zebra. Figures crossing between the youth in the van and the constable on the island cause the movements of the latter to appear, at moments, ambivalent: the youth does not dare remove his eyes. Too, from the concave seat below the flower boxes she could see, along Pike Street, the obelisk and the sea – the obelisk, the promenade, and the sea, more precisely speaking. Her husband did not feel he wished to tire her with the long walk up the hill for the tram station.

Everyone agrees that this walk is tiring. Besides which the practically vertical ascent of the little tram groaning on its cables would be too much for a pregnant woman; she couldn't reasonably be expected to stand the gnashing, the grinding, the little tram climbing, leaving below the workers' cottages at the foot of the hill, their purple roofs, cutting through fields dotted with sheep, past areas of wild combed grass that seem smoking in the wind, up the rock, penetrating the lashing wind which blows now from remote horizons – powerful, silent, without resistance – above the accustomed eyeline to define the bay in new perspectives, Sweeley Street a row of jagged roofs crawling towards unfamiliar vanishing points, towards the rocks; the Shore Road and the Promenade bracing the bay, holding for two miles, perhaps three, a rough parallel with the streets scored like wounds across the face of the town, the town itself resolved into an orderly pattern of roofs – orange, gold, black – bounded by the hills, the river, the bay bulging inland in an expansive flat crescent pinned at its ends to the twin spurs of Trwyn Mawr and Trwyn Bach. Then Caedmon Castle, the bridge, the railway tunnel, mussel banks black in the tide, white clusters marking caravan sites along the west bank of the river, the Straits of Môn. Beetle Island, the Isle of Môn, then the ocean, the North Atlantic – mediterranean blue just now flecked with white, with diminutive breakers that seem never to move. At the head of Sweeley Street, by the roundabout, the traffic has condensed for the zebra, waiting – a controlled crossing, a jewelled figure in the stream of pedestrians immobile on an island. From the remotest distance, from the Great Western Hotel, all is motion, advancing, receding, occupying the main directions of his view though he cannot be unaware, from moment to moment, of activity more close at hand, on either side, at the heads of the zebra. He pivots, beckoning this way and that to the crowd mainly concentrated, at this cool hour, on the sunny side of the street.

And the rock itself looked at from Sweeley Street? From Sweeley Street, from the roundabout where stands the bronze figure of the Welsh martyr, the landward end of the rock pushes all the houses up the slope into a gentle elevation not obvious for the wood that clothes the foot of the spur, but which is violently there, looking higher, in the layered formation of rockseams rising and buckling out of the earth.

From Sweeley Street, from the roundabout, one does not notice the vertical drop which the rock takes into the sea. From Sweeley Street all that it is possible to see, substantially, is Sweeley Street: from the Great Western to the rock, from the rock to the Great Western. Along this stretch of street a cambridge-blue delivery van is nosing its way out of Banks Mews laden with the day's deliveries. Banks Press, Job Printers, Photo Engravers, Commercial Designers, *The Cambrian Weekly Record.* Near the roundabout, at Pike Street, Sean leaps out of a fish-shop: Hey! and his smell of stale beer nearly knocks me flat. Reflected in the show window of the chemist's opposite, the encounter – collision it might more properly be called, for I spin about facing him – looks like this: Two men meet at a corner on a busy street in a seaside town, one not yet thirty, the other middle aged. The younger man wears a gaberdine mac belted so tightly that he is shaped rather like an up-ended cello, what with his broad shoulders and the drainpipe slacks following the contour of his legs to the broken-down black shoes. In one hand he carries a paper bag, the other is in his pocket. Tall, fresh brooding face, gingery hair. Talking to him the older man looks past his shoulder at their joint reflections, their images steady as rocks in the stream of passers-by. The pale blue anorak, the corduroys, the worn suede boots which the older man wears are partly obscured by the silhouette of his friend, who now opens the bag – there is a blue trade name on it which from a distance (two widths of Sweeley Street) it is impossible to read – and offers its contents, talking the while. The expression on his face likewise is not visible, but his movements are earnest, even intense. His great mop of hair flutters occasionally in the wind. The older man's face is amiably incredulous; from time to time he tosses his head sideways doubtingly, amused. There is, however, something penetratingly watchful about his expression, and this has stamped all his features with the tired concentration sometimes observable among railway engine drivers or airline pilots. Now his face breaks into a laugh which, across the double width of Sweeley Street, is soundless.

The pregnant woman in the pink smock stops in front of the chemist's window just as a green double-decker pulling in to the kerb causes the reflections there to vanish. Persons on the lower deck of this bus can observe two men sharing the contents of a paper bag, pedestrians moving behind them. The younger man is not taken aback by unsympathetic laughter; he seems even to be unaware of it. He is insisting: Don't bother telling me the world's a lousy hole, I know when I'm licked all right.

Don't be such a clot Sean, she's sure to be back.

Because that's what you said last time, remember – a rotten lousy hole, remember?

And you'll have a jolly little party afterwards and bash me around a bit again.

Worse things happen to people for less you know, much worse.

But you just can't help inviting your friends around for a bashing every now and then, can you! Bags of remorse to chew on afterwards, eh?

Had enough of this bloody hole, that's what it is, enough; don't know how you stand it. She's felt it too, a long time – it had to happen; I'm going home.

The double-decker grinds on; the mute play can again be observed in the chemist's window. But now the pregnant woman in the pink smock gazes at a showcard of a luminous irregularly pointed star in which colours glow and vanish in measured cycles – an advertising gadget which has held her attention for some minutes. Occasionally her eyes wander over the rest of the showcase but without taking in the mass of feminine trivia banked there almost to the ceiling; they return again and again to the kaleidoscopic colour burning itself to blackness in each point of the star only to flower again as the cycle returns. Over her head, in dozens of postures, a blonde figure appears, now in mink, now in mist, now in a foamy bath, now reflected in a million mirrors, now nude among floating bubbles, now her hair, her eyes, now bare legs, pelvis bare, augmented breasts.

This is what the pregnant woman is wearing: pink and white, not a pink, smock – white with pink stripes that shimmer and seem wholly pink. But it isn't a smock since she's wearing nothing under it, apparently; a sack rather, full, gathered, falling from a cape with bits of lace around this cape and on the pockets. No sleeves. Bare arms, pink and white. The pink stripes vibrating discharge a complementary violet into the white so that at a certain distance the garment isn't, strictly speaking, white or pink, but mauve. At various distances the pregnant woman therefore wears a pink smock, a pink and white, or a mauve, depending on the locus of observation.

From a locus by Masons the Shoe Shop, it can be anticipated that the man now carelessly leaving the kerb will have an accident.

Without splitting hairs proximity can be said to make all the difference in the case of the smock – pink, pink and white, mauve – within a radius of sixty yards, eighty at most, beyond which of course it becomes increasingly grey. But in the case of her shoes, handbag, shopping-basket this is not so: within a reasonable radius these remain the same plain grey, brown, gold, from any point of view. From near at hand however the footwear proves to be neither shoes nor slippers but a type of sneakers, creepers, or moccasins made of imitation skin and not of leather at all as might have been thought from farther away. Then the man leaving the kerb some distance off with his eyes on the poster across the way – the poster of a golden blonde – collides with a tramp bending over the gutter intent apparently on recovering some discarded trifle there. Why the bloody hell don't you look where y'going? This man's face in the slanting sunlight seems lilac, of a chalky texture.

What she sees reflected in the show window are the two men chewing greedily, the older tossing the contents of the bag from his palms to his mouth in an almost continuous manner. The preoccupation with the food causes him to seem off-hand; he stares about casually, greeting this friend and that, while the food apparently warms his insides, for presently he begins to eat less ravenously and appears even to be attending to what the other is saying.

Sean is saying: That's a new caper she's onto now you know – swiping my frenchies whenever she chooses to skedaddle.

I mouth a shape that means: Bitch! but a shrimp pops out; I try to catch it – only one hand is free, the other holds the paper bag – it rolls off the kerb and comes to rest near the heels of a man nearby – a tramp straddling the gutter. Simultaneously someone stepping carelessly off the kerb, a man with a lilac complexion, collides with this tramp; they embrace each other for support. Why the bloody hell don't you look where y'going? Then the smell of sweat joins that of stale beer. The kerbstones, dimpled rectangular blocks, are of granite from the Caedmon quarries.

Same's last time, isn't it – swiping my frenchies; I've had enough, I won't stand it anymore.

So I advise a clean break, that's always best. It is impossible ever to know another person really, especially a woman. It is the old old problem – holding a woman is a creative act, he should realise, for which few of us are particularly well equipped. But he regards me defensively: the solution doesn't appeal to him at all.

The Mini-van incredibly is still inching towards the row of studs that marks the zebra. Now the fingers of the youth are drumming against the door. In gaps between figures on the crossing the youth can see two men, one in a gaberdine mac, the other in a blue anorak, talking. Nearby a shabby figure straddling the gutter examines the kerbstones, or even perhaps searches for some trifle there.

Another bus pulling in across the way isolates us in the jumble of the holiday crowd. A few paces off the constable can be heard to object: What's the use me being here? to the pregnant woman in the pink smock – pink and white at this distance – who has waddled onto the traffic island beside him and stands there experimentally peering into the compact line of vehicles: If you go skippin' through movin' traffic any'ow, eh? The woman looks chastened; her very fair, freckled face reddens. The constable beckons to the other half of the zebra and persons begin spilling onto the crossing. He says: Hurry along there, lass! to a pair of tubby legs in black shorts and plimsolls which then step off the island and become entangled in a rapid pattern of scissoring X's in the tail of his eye, at that moment fixed on the windscreen of a Morris 1100 where a small tongue is pressed between spread-eagled fingers. He watches the heads thin out around him, brings the vehicles on in the down lane, signals the up lane, watches wheels spin across the zebra, irregular leaping shadows, pebbles glittering in the tarmac then, his gaze a good half-circle off and at that moment vaguely caught by a bouncing beach ball slung in a yellow string bag some distance away, he sees, quite close to the zebra, in the foreground, almost on the kerbstones, two men deep in conversation, one wearing a blue anorak and corduroys, the other a tightly belted gaberdine mac. In the gaps that open and close in the traffic he notes that they are engrossed with the contents of a paper bag – cream with blue lettering – which passes between them. A young girl with a spotted beach ball in a nylon string bag has reached the head of the zebra in full sunlight and stands there flicking her knees out alternately to maintain its rhythmic bouncing. She has come to a stop not far from the two men but neither is aware of the other. Around the girl persons begin to accumulate, eyes on the constable who just for the moment has given his attention wholly to the traffic. On eye level the lower deck of a bus rips past swallowing all other sound, flattening the constable's picture; immediate panels of serial faces unreel against his nose, vanish expressionless, followed by a dazzling gap of sunlight in which a peach-coloured after-image impinges on the fragmentary picture of the small group waiting on the left hand pavement by the zebra, an indeterminate mass, the girl still bouncing the beach ball, the pair of men with the paper bag still conversing, another serial blur of faces as a follow-ing bus accelerates, instant of a hand plunged into the paper bag, the gaberdine mac, a cycling club progressively overtaken appear-ing and disappearing in irregular sequence – yellow stripes and black – boys, girls, wheels, spokes, pedals, knees circling, per-spective discs dwindling, banking like planes in unison down the hill past the Odeon for the curve at Parry Road by St John's, their last silhouettes caught in the glass of Orion Telectrics then smack! concealed by the façade of the fire station towering against the blue. There a miasmic blur for a moment remains in which distant figures seem to crawl. But close at hand, at the ends of the zebra, on each pavement, the pressure has once again built up. On the right side of the constable, in the shadow cast by Cassels the Stationers, an indeterminate group of persons, none of whose faces retain his attention (though some are familiar); on his left another indeterminate group in which are the young girl bouncing a beach ball in alternate rhythms against her knees, the pregnant woman in a pink and white or mauve smock and the two men – one in a light blue anorak, the other in a gaberdine mac – still deep in conversation. He brings the traffic to a halt, releases both knots of impatient faces. Above the hurrying heads tower the shoulders of the man in the gaberdine mac whose reddish hair just flutters in the wind, bent over, intent on the paper bag.

I point out to Sean the hoarding over the pavement on the opposite side of the street where a blonde bitch rides high on a famous brand of motorcar tyre, rubber and flesh skilfully modelled, where across the face of the double quad-crown poster appears the caption: IT'S UP TO YOU! Long golden legs dangle over the heads of passers-by. But he objects:

I've had enough chum, know when I'm licked.

For a moment I feel he's grasped the protest which I mouth, but clearly his mind is elsewhere. This is what I have said: Isn't right, you know, stimulating the public like that, is it! Young boys and girls, you know, not right. Teenagers today –

But simultaneously above the traffic roar St John's chimes the Elevation of the Host: clong…clong…clong… a sound which would clearly be heard in Banks Mews behind the church, in the concrete courtyard away from the machine clatter, where just now the cambridge-blue delivery van – Banks Press, Job Printers, Photo Engravers, Commercial Designers, *The Cambrian Weekly Record* – is being loaded for the day's rounds, and would any moment now nose its way out of the mews to join the traffic along Sweeley Street obliquely opposite the point where the jet-age goddess dangles golden legs over the heads of passers-by, where traffic decelerates and condenses for the roundabout at Pike

Street, where from the concave benches below the level of the flower boxes the pregnant woman gazes at the obelisk, the promenade, the sea. From this position only the last few inches of sea can be seen beyond the promenade wall below the line of horizon. Motorcars parked in the open space surrounding the obelisk form an island around which the traffic flows in three directions – along the promenade, into Pike Street, towards the rock.

And nothing to it when all's said and done either. No, I've bloody well had enough.

Suit yourself, chum.

Couldn't feel the same again, no not me, what's she take me for?

Fair enough.

No, won't be had again, not bloody worth it, is it?

Anything in the world's worth a good piece of fanny, Sean, way I see it, anything in this world. What else is there?

Then the third group of three chimes from the twin steeples of St John's expires in the traffic roar. Sean looks up at a cluster of seagulls that have just spattered the pavement; he examines his mac. Again the constable brings the traffic to a halt, pivoting. Then beneath him the pregnant woman commences the second half of the crossing, beyond the traffic island. In the shadow falling from Cassels the Stationers, Est. 1898, is the image of the powerful neck, the pale blue collar, the fit of the tunic about his shoulders. She gains the kerbstones with short quick steps as the traffic begins crawling forward. A windtone horn barks in a rage nearby, the train of vehicles stops, chain-like. A grey blur regains the pavement, forms itself under the eye of the constable into the figure of a repentant jay-walker, which eye he keeps fixed on that quaking person, enjoying it, until the traffic moves once more. The jay-walker comes up short against Sean's massive shoulders. Need one's wits around here, don't one!

That'sfact!

And from behind a woman exclaims: 'Ere, you just try that once more and I'll. There is a scream of fright. I look around. A bawling. The child is walking at an acute backward angle straining against his mother. On the opposite pavement is a young girl idly rotating a stand of seaside postcards, bouncing a spotted beach ball in a nylon string bag in alternate rhythms against her knees. By the kerb the pregnant woman in the pink smock turns from gazing at the constable's hairy neck and enters the butcher's, which lies in a straight line from the zebra, next to the chemist's.

S'what you up to now – where y'going?

People think they can possess your soul don't they, or what?

They can. Where y'going?

Dunno; get some sleep I expect. Where *you* going?

I shrug. Bust up with the wife you know, last night.

He doesn't move; he seems reluctant, perhaps even afraid to. Yet he doesn't enjoy staying.

I'd have a party all right if she comes back; be nice won't it, have a little party?

Her lido-green eyes Sean, that's what gets me, I don't mind admitting, that and the jet-black hair. Coo! If you hadn't've come barging out into the corridor that night, you know –

See what I mean, now don't you, see what I mean then?

He is angry. The natural focus of his vision, gazing straight ahead, is the star glowing in cyclic rhythms in the chemist's window opposite. To the left of this the beach ball bouncing on the young girl's knees forms a visual limit of which he must be aware, though this does not hold his attention. The figure of the constable on the island forms a similar limit on his right, but just at the moment, so far as it is possible to tell, his gaze is centred on the iridescent star. Vehicles of every description penetrate his middle distance and vanish to the left and to the right. These of course he sees, but neither notes nor observes; it is beyond his interest for instance to discriminate between the several makes of motorcars that come and go, or even to distinguish between their respective colours. Possibly he sees nothing at all, at this moment, of the substance of Sweeley Street; the images which impinge on his eyes perhaps altogether fail to register on his mind. It is not until the rhythm of the traffic is broken by two dark figures obliquely crossing the street that he shifts his gaze from the show window. Two girls in bell-bottom jeans and black oilskin jackets have gained the centre of the street and pause there a moment negotiating the oncoming stream of traffic. Locks of curly brown hair flutter about their shoulders as they stand, arm in arm, awaiting a gap. One head, higher than the other, just reaches to the bottom line of the hoarding across the way, below the dangling legs of the blonde on the motorcar tyre. More cars go by before traffic is held up at the zebra further along to the right. But from their movements as they gain the opposite pavement it becomes obvious that one of the pair is not a girl but a youth, a year or two older perhaps than his companion. It is possible to follow their figures only in glimpses as they edge and dodge through the crowd towards the library. Just as he loses sight of them in that direction Sean becomes for the first time aware, apparently, next to an election poster, of the golden blonde across whose bare torso is written the caption: IT'S UP TO YOU! white on a blue ground, though UP, a little larger than its fellows, is finished in yellow. An ordinary advertisement, easily interchange-able with many another for various other products, as are also the aspect and appeal of the blonde who is its central motif. But the ambivalence of the copy is striking: IT'S **UP** TO YOU! The emphasis on the second word makes of it a phrase which is entirely new, familiar as it is, implying, obviously, quality: up to your taste, your judgement, fastidiousness, et cetera. But omit-ting the emphasis and reading it in the ordinary way – difficult on account of the contrasted word – the phrase, as it does every day in every kind of context, simply suggests a choice, the subject of the choice being, in this case, the boldly displayed trade name of the tyre presented: POLYPLEX. Why hadn't it been left at that – why the equivoque?

Why can't a man be left alone?

She'll never do that; no, not after what you've done to her. You haven't heard the last of it chum; that's what the bitches do – exact a price.

On the edge of the pavement, at the spot just crossed by the teenage couple, stands a man with a lilac complexion, hands in the pockets of his dog-tooth check jacket, staring up the pavement, and down. His figure is in shadow from the buildings behind him. Even so it is possible to distinguish the outline of a paper rose stuck in his lapel, above the heart. The shadow of Sean's profile on the pinkish flagstones is picked up momentarily against the clothes of passers-by and let fall; it behaves like a puppet, blathering, changing stance, changing colour with each garment it falls upon, crazily changing shape with the density of the crowd so that at times it stands nearby, erect, another Sean down to the heavy brows, the large overhanging nose; at others, in full sunlight, merely a blob of head rises ghoul-like against someone's trouser legs or nylons. Two girls and a youth come to an idle stop beside him, gaze into the window of Masons the Shoe Shop nearby. A public house on the roundabout (The County), next to that Woolworths, then a Tobacconists (Lewis), Premier Fisheries, then Masons – that's how near we stand to the constable and the zebra. The awning is out over Premier Fisheries but not over Masons, so that the slanting sunlight draws reddish bristles from the surface of Sean's skin along one half of his face, framing a pale, luminous almost transparent eye whose pupil is reduced to a pinhead in the glare; the other eye is veiled in shadow.

Just look at that bit of bitch across the way, Sean, there – in the butcher's door: pink smock, no mauve; bet she can't keep off it even now.

The two girls leave Masons and drift towards the head of the zebra. They wear Welsh costume – black funnel hats, brown skirts, blouses, aprons, long black boots with silver clasps. The trays they carry are filled with paper roses of the kind exchanged for charities in public places.

What's biting you, Joss?

How?

Jumpy today. Why?

In the butcher's doorway the pregnant woman is agitated; flushed, she stands beside the butcher who has come from behind the counter to finish their conversation at the door. His face is cracked and yellowed, like old ivory, and as impassive. They observe two men on the opposite pavement who are clearly staring at them, maybe passing remarks: one in a pale blue anorak and corduroys, and the other in a gaberdine mac.

It's her father's done that to her you know, Joss.

What – warmed up her fanny?

Fathers can affect a girl – he's the only man in her life, you know.

What about all the others?

Doesn't feel a thing; I know she doesn't.

He should be hung, the sod.

The woman thinks it disgusting, they've done nothing but stare at her wherever she's been all the morning; it oughtn't to be allowed. The butcher knows Joss Banks, the printer, the older man, the one in the blue jacket – Brummagen or something, Londoner maybe. Been around years. Suddenly sold up his business and running to seed, but harmless, quite harmless.

So indeed he seems; not harmless merely, but respectable – a schoolmaster, professional man. Not unattractive, too, in his face-worn way. The woman doubts – she might be imagining things. She moves on next door, to the chemist's. But before entering the shop she pauses once more in front of the show window observing the reflections, watching the star exploding and expiring to its mechanical pulse. What she sees there is that the two men have shifted their positions away from the oblique so that the axis of their gaze makes a right angle with the direction of Sweeley Street; its natural focus is now the star in the chemist's window opposite where, across the double width of the street they can see reflected themselves, the constable on his island, the zebra, a woman in a mauve smock, crowds on both pavements, traffic in between.

Sure seems to be loitering, doesn't she? Wonder why?

And my eyes fall, not far from where she stands, on the figure of a small girl with a polka-dot beach ball in a yellow string bag who has collected half a dozen or so seaside postcards from a rotary display stand outside the paper shop next to the chemist's and begins moving through the door, arms enquiringly raised shoulder high. From time to time the woman turns to observe in the flesh, on the pavement opposite, some image whose reflection she has not clearly read in the window. She observes without noting, that two girls in Welsh costume have just commenced crossing the zebra, flower trays on their slender waists; she sees also two or three obtruding colours in the crowd, PREMIER FISHERIES in blue somewhere on a white ground, two striped pillars marking the traffic island, the two men talking. SNACKS. The zebra.

The constable.

It is an attitude whose simple lack of guile arrests the attention of the constable on his island, for nothing interposes itself between the thoughts of the small girl and her actions. Finished with her scrutiny of the blatantly nasty pictures she now holds them in a manner, clear of her body, that acknowledges their ownership until the last moment, when she would have paid for them. As she disappears through the door of the paper shop the pregnant woman turns, once more facing the show window. She is followed, the constable observes, by a young woman, obviously not a local, in a transparent mac of a pale blue colour – a colour which lingers in his mind for it is that of the anorak worn by the middle-aged man on the opposite pavement standing in conversation with a friend in a gaberdine mac, gazing reflectively across the road.

Nearly half killed the bitch last night, if you want to know.

But Sean doesn't; doesn't so much as hear.

What the bloody hell makes women that way then?

His attention is focused on Orion Telectrics where, on the pavement, a Levantine salesman demonstrates a portable tape recorder. Vehicles parked on either side of the road prevent buses approaching the roundabout in the direction of Trwyn Mawr from pulling in to the kerb, at this point Sweeley Street not being very wide, no more than thirty feet across at most: obviously not conceived for the present volume of traffic. About this, later in the day, the publican at The County complains: Sweeley Street should be made one-way – it never was meant for the present volume of traffic. All there'd been along there fifty years ago was the odd horse bus, the few coaches and that: no macadam, no pavements, nothing of the kind. People were more careful – the old street vendors, flower sellers and so on, they felt safe; every morning you could find the cabbies hanging around the watering troughs down there by where the Great Western Hotel now stands, discussing the day; your life was not in anybody else's hands, except you worried about the talk of war and that.

Sounds of traffic, of seagulls, provide a background rich in texture for the foreign salesman demonstrating the range of his instrument. Against this background, which is not effectually a background at all but an audible manifestation as it were of the life around in which he himself seems but a livid instant, he extemporises a commentary after the manner of a radio commentator. The effect is curious, the man's voice becoming only in lulls in the general hubbub the locus or centre of an articulate space, a position commanded at other times by the haphazard shriek of seagulls, the babble of the crowd, the barking of dogs, by various mechanical sounds, all of which, advancing, receding, seem to possess the man at least to the degree in which he possesses them; his utterances are its utterances, extending beyond himself, his meaning. Why though does the pregnant woman stare so intently into the show window of the chemist's?

The person with the lilac complexion has disappeared.

She notes that the two men have again begun talking across the way, but their attention is now on the constable.

Sean has the build of a policeman.

This chap's got nothing on you has he, the Force needs men. Forget the woman.

As he eases another dense spill of the crowd across the zebra the constable's attention is fixed momentarily on two men by the kerb, one in a pale blue anorak, the other in a gaberdine mac. Along the opposite pavement, under the hoarding but backing it, is a man with a lilac complexion, hands stuffed into his pockets. But standing at that spot now is a family with a pushchair gauging the traffic: he is no longer to be seen. Some distance off, in front of the library, a youth with shoulder-length hair has just dragged his girl out of the phone box. They walk in the direction of the Great Western but abruptly in front of the Odeon they cross the street to look at the picture placards displayed there. From a distance male and female are indistinguishable.

The Great Western closes the perspective at the bottom end of Sweeley Street behind the park – a park provided with swings, a fountain, and public lavatories. At the triangle formed by this park the traffic divides, one arm continuing along the upper reaches of Sweeley Street where the shopping centre comes to an end at Electric House. There the road runs past the football ground and the field where the Gwyddr Fair is up for the season; at Llanwrog, the next village along the coast, it joins the Shore Road which at one end circles the foot of Trwyn Bach, at the other plunges into a tunnel through the heart of Trwyn Mawr. The other arm of traffic turns along the right side of the triangle in front of the Great Western to run inland along the river into the hills.

The salesman's foreign patter has gathered a few persons around him, one or two of whom he invites to join his commentary; but the small crowd is mistrustful. Persons look at him as upon a man set apart by extraordinary talents, as on a conjurer say, or a circus rider. This is due to his alien and unemotive observation of the minutiae of Sweeley Street, much as though it were a living thing – the appearance of flats and hotels above the rows of shops, the shapes of their windows, the condition of the plaster, colour of curtains, the painted or gold-lettered signs of first-floor businesses: solicitors, hairdressers, dentists, et cetera, things which in their familiar comings and goings they have never suspected to be there. Now with satisfaction, even with wonder, they verify the observations of this stranger; they point to his omissions, which in the nature of things are many.

The commentary ends with a general description of the monument: the feverish attenuated figure of the great Welshman (1856-1924) who sacrificed himself for the planting of Christianity in Darkest Africa. Greater love hath no man than this. *Mewn Hedd!*

Mewn Hedd! In the foreign accent the words cling – the dead sometimes do not rest in peace. In the striking sunlight a person here and there on the fringe of the crowd can be seen with unctuous concern to cross himself, but no more notice is taken of this generally than of the sound of the bells of St John's which now for some reason have once more commenced chiming, fugally cascading, vibrating in the black towers silhouetted against the sky, finally expiring in the drift that whispers through the town.

A portion of sky is disturbed. Clouds rent by remote agitations. It is, one remembers, St Swithin's – but elsewhere all is smiling blue, a blue which darkens the colour of the ocean and permeates the shadows now commencing to creep backwards across Sweeley Street. In these shadows the clothes of pedestrians too are modified in colour so that the dresses of two women who now appear at the rotary display stand outside the paper shop seem mauve and grey instead of pink and white respectively. The younger of these two women, who wears a cone of frothy white hair the texture of candy floss, nods from time to time in apparent sympathy with some complaint addressed to her by her companion, the pregnant woman. She throws sidelong glances across the road to where two men on the kerb, one young, the other older in a blue anorak, are shielding their eyes and gazing into the sky. Following their gaze she sees, thousands of feet up, a double trail of vapour scored against the blue by two points of light glinting like distant stars. When his eyes return to Sweeley Street very many persons are staring upwards – two bus queues in front of Marks and Spencers, a small group farther down in front of Orion Telectrics, a scatter of persons by St John's. The teenage couple leave the foyer of the Odeon, eyes on the pavement. An immaterial pink tracery still hops in loops and arcs across his vision and this from the island afloat in dense sunlight changes to crimson, then to violet, into dots and clusters of purple like free forget-me-nots, then into a mass of mauve that comes to rest in front of the paper shop in the shape of two women beside the rotary display stand, immobile, staring at the salesman winding the flex of his microphone. He makes his way through a battery of placarded washing machines lining the doorway, into the shop. One or two persons follow, with backward English glances.

Sure, give her a dose of her own medicine is what I say.

Oddly though, it is the last thing Sean wishes to do.

Give you my address then, case you want to write.

He shoves a hand into the pocket of his mac, brings out a paperback novel in which is stuck a nasty postcard. Two persons, male and female, are leaving a wood, almost naked, under a stormy sky. The caption reads: RAIN STOPPED PLAY.

That's a funny one, that, about this painter and his girl. Gives up his family and all, painting space you know, pure space... got a pen or something?

For a few pence a ballpoint can be purchased in Woolworths. Which should take no more time than it costs to climb to the first floor, to the stationery counter. The salesgirl there is charming to Sean, dilatory, who doesn't notice. Pretty in a lilac dustcoat which is too full, too long, her inquiry is addressed to him though it is I, I make clear, who will make the purchase. (It is the same in Boots', some minutes later, where he gets some Codeine tablets for a feeling in the head.) These incidents obviously do not merit the depression they cause, but the feeling is there just the same. The girl's dustcoat might be pale rose or even yellow (ochre, saffron, citron, lime): what tricks the memory plays! Most striking is the ease with which her torso succeeds in impressing itself upon the garment, despite its fullness. The same is noticeable, though less remarkable, about the figure of the pregnant woman inside the pink and white, or pink, or mauve smock – from the contour of her thighs as the wind moulds the material of the dress around them while I cross her crossing the zebra, to the brooding curvature of her back across the shoulders, the slope of the shoulders, the high position of her breasts, which are rather wide apart. Even reflected in the butcher's window as the constable leans over listening to her, something can be said too about the steep angle of her pelvic bone with the resulting obtrusion of the cotyledonous buttocks, the back of the figure seeming strangely not complementary to the front; from the show window, but for her straddling gait as she approaches the constable, it is difficult to be certain that the woman is pregnant at all. It is obvious that the salesgirl's ivory breasts depend from rather hollow collar-bones and grow smoothly into the rest of her torso with no trace at all of a fold and no need therefore of any form of support. The same can be said of the straight flat back, spatulate buttocks, narrow hips: they are all of a piece with her flexible limbs, like an octopus.

There is such a variety of types among the ballpoints that Sean is some time making up his mind. He adds his doodles to innumerable others on a scribbling pad provided for the purpose, testing, selecting, rejecting, for no other reason apparently than that choice is possible. They all behave in the same unpredictable way – a single stroke producing an initial absence of ink in defiance of pressure or persistence followed by an erratic granular trace and a viscous blob that almost binds pen to paper. There seems to be some difference though in the relative viscosity of the inks depending on their colour; the more fluid, the more tractable and consistent of them appear to go with those colours that are the most useless, with red and green for example. The more useful, blue or black, are the least dependable, the most unpleasant.

The extent of the visual field is determined by the four walls of the building though inside Woolworths it is difficult to speak of walls at all: there is merely a limit to the impression of brilliant objects extending in every direction, relieved, to the east and to the west, by windows opening onto Sweeley Street on the one hand, and onto an alleyway in which is a timber yard on the other. Under my baggy stare the salesgirl falters, momentarily repersonalised, then speaks loudly to Sean, but pen in hand Sean is watching the cretins approach, each bearing his paper rose, even the chaperon or teacher, an earthy navvy-like individual with no trace of dedication in his face or manner and a rough sensible way with the boys. The scribbling pad is covered with doodles which, but for the variety of colours in which they are drawn, all look the same: mostly curvilinear and centripetal with dwindling tails that invariably fade horizontally – to the right, indecipherable signatures, an addition sum whose total, 12/9, is wrong. With some effort a popular tune can be discerned on the amplifiers above the hubbub of the shopping crowd. At rest the salesgirl's childish lips are uneasy. Approaching, the cretins bump into persons along the pavement, shoulders first, oblique, knees sagging, arms dangling, grinning. As we stare one of them sticks his paper rose (of the type exchanged for donations to public charities) into my hand, and laughs unpleasantly. Sean says nothing. With a degree of concentration, as though forcing himself to remember, or possibly to visualise, it, he writes his address: Infirmary Street, Dublin, then warns: Only it won't be any use after next weekend, I'll be travelling. Grudgingly he gives it to me, then stuffs the novel, which is called *Brigand*, back into his mac pocket. Time you get to chapter five you realise the chap's a man with a briefcase only *dreaming* he's an artist, see? That's the point, see – a thief. Brigand, see. Terribly clever. Because it's stopping him in his marriage and everything, if y'see what I mean, and that's the main thing, isn't it!

Isn't it!

At last the young girl considers the purchase made: the post-cards are hers. Leaving, she encounters a blonde woman in a blue plastic mac who slips by sideways into the shop, whose fragrance of body or hair leaves a suggestion of freshly mown corn. Out of the corner of his eye the constable perhaps registers a blue sensation dissolving into the gloom of the paper shop as the child with the postcards emerges still carrying the spotted beach ball but now he pays no attention to her for persons have again accumulated at both ends of the zebra, waiting. It is too late to refer this marginal blue sensation to any recognisable impression: the constable does not try in any case for simultaneously he becomes aware that the two men have disappeared from the pavement. The mass of Trwyn Mawr bares the rhythm of its rockseams to the roofs of hotels along its base. Far below, from the obelisk on Pike Street, two schoolboys scrutinise its surface through field glasses for fossils presumably, or for the birds' nests which are the subject of their dangerous sport each summer.

Considering the purchase made (he has rejected both the Aspirin and the Disprin tablets and reads now the small type on the Codeine label), the girl looks once more into Sean's grey eyes with a flirtatious smile. Sean is good looking but needs a shave, a wash, a shampoo, some general grooming. He remains unaware of his effect on the girl who, in the chemical light and synthetic atmosphere inside Boots', seems waxlike. Then he hands the pen back to me, which I stick into my pocket. In this pocket is Sandra's postcard of Marquet's *Beach Carnival.* I show it to Sean: Here, cheer yourself up, lovely bit of skin, that! But he isn't interested in the purple nude with a bare leg raised against the rock, though the colour is exquisite against the pearly grey. There is also of course the suggestiveness of the juxtaposition of female flesh with granite. It is a painting by a very minor *Fauve* and not good, but the carnival theme interests me. Sean hands it back: Old flame in Paris then or something?

I am flattered, though I have to admit that the card is not from an old flame but from my stepdaughter, Sandra, just honey-mooning there. Remember Lho don't you, Lawrence Henry Owen, the commercial artist? His daughter, you know –

Sean knows all right, remembers, says nothing. A sonic boom rocks Sweeley Street. Again people look into the sky. An orange-coloured RAF trainer is visible against the blue below the old double line of vapour which now is shredded, torn, cast adrift behind a rising cumulus. He says: Haven't been the same man since, have you Joss?

I'd be the last to know that, wouldn't I now?

Y'haven't y'know, admit it.

Chris'sake, who's the same after anything! Use your blooming nut, who's to say – same's what anyway?

None my business; no need to shout. None my business, old man.

None of anybody's, all these people, shite, I'm not losing me sleep over Lho; *they* haven't been the same either, who's to judge, who's to bloody well say, tell me!

When the blonde bitch leaves the paper shop across the way she is no longer wearing the mac; her hair falls just short of the shoulder blades, which the neckline of the summer frock leaves bare. She walks in the same direction as everyone else on that pavement: up the street towards the roundabout. The show window of the shop which reflects my solitary figure on the kerb, as well as the enormous new building behind me, is identical with that of the shop next door, and the one next to that, and the next one. All the shops are the same, in fact, in the pair of mammoth steel and glass constructions that run the length of Sweeley Street on either side, straddling the lesser streets, alleys, and mews with cantilevered archways. They are not really separate shops at all but one super shop with show windows separated from each other by revolving doors that never pause in their mechanical rotation. The plan of these doors is star-shaped rather than cruciform, allowing a minimal space for each individual, so that their efficient use calls for quick wits and extreme caution. Nevertheless the crowd pours in and out with the greatest apparent ease and fluidity, even quite small children, entrances and exits alternating as far as the eye can see in either direction. In either direction the crowd swarms all one way – up Sweeley Street towards the rock, or down Sweeley Street towards the park. Seemingly on an impulse she disappears through one of the revolving doors.

I'm not losing me sleep over Lho – I can tell you that.

No bus pulls in to sever image from referent, shadow from substance. There is no traffic, naturally, because of the convection domes that span the street every hundred yards along or so. The crowd does not step off the kerb even so, but follows the prescribed direction ever to the right – up Sweeley Street towards Trwyn Mawr on one side of the road, and on the other, the side where I stand, down the street towards the park behind which, in the old days, used to stand the Great Western Hotel.

Sean crushes a letter between his fists in sudden exasperation, then goes through the action of tossing it into the gutter: an outward flicking of the elbow and a counter-clockwise twirling of the fingers, but the letter remains balled in one hand. The blonde bitch leaves one doorway and enters another, searching, apparently, for some unobtainable commodity, for a child, or even a man. The latter seems not unlikely for, assuming that she knows what it is she wants to purchase, there is no need for her to leave the building – all her wants can be satisfied there, in one department or another. For a while I think that it is the paper bag from the boiled shrimps which he has treated in this way, flicking it off from his right side with the action of a spin bowler; but the paper bag is already there, crumpled in the gutter, identifiable by traces of the blue trade name – PREMIER FISHERIES – still here and there visible across the fissures, the creases and shadows of the ball. A faint smell of burnt petrol rises from the kerb. This escapes from the nearest convection dome a few yards off, near where the library once stood. This faint but continuous odour from the traffic below is what mainly keeps people off the streets; the direction of their movement, constantly to the right, is explained by the position of the various surface stations at points along the pavements by means of which these people communicate with the traffic below: ingress along one side, egress by the other. No one would dream of questioning the arrangement. But Sean has not just crumpled the paper bag; he had done that, I seem to remember, even before the cretins went by or before he began talking about the paperback novel (whichever is prior) still sticking out of his pocket, a tiny blue triangle of it just visible against that portion of the gaberdine mac around the pocket where the material from constant use is frayed, blackened, glassy. I'm sick to death of stories, I tell him. I don't want to read another story ever, what's the use; the most remarkable stories remain locked up inside each man impossible of telling – no one would dare. It is meant provocatively, to prevent him depressing me further, to protect myself: I do not wish to be depressed, I prefer to be deaf to his worries like the crowd in docile locomotion on the far side of the street which, now that the traffic problem has been solved, has no further use for the constables perched in transparent sentry boxes one on each of the metal convection domes. The constables, notwithstanding, have been multiplied along the street, for even greater vigilance is now needed against the vestigial wilfulness of some individuals. This change in the role of the policeman is no more apparent, it would seem, to the average member of the crowd than is any change observable in himself, for it is matter only that is subject to change, one is prone to think, and not man. I'm sick to the teeth of stories, believe me; I never want to read another – ever!

The cretins file out of the snack bar, as before contained by the rudest solicitude on the part of their chaperon or teacher. A jocular familiarity prevails nevertheless between man and master; they understand one another. The sanctions for his authority are doubtless terrible beyond measure. Yet freely and without interference on his part they distribute their roses to all and sundry, even scattering them around the bronze feet of the Welsh martyr on his pedestal.

And why does the woman in the pink smock gaze so intently into the show window of the chemist's?

Then the cycling club goes by, boys and girls, yellow stripes and black, pedalling down the hill.

IT'S **UP** TO YOU!

The woman in the pink, pink and white, or mauve smock gazes into the show window, into the very heart or very eye of the spectral star where darkness fathers the colours of the world, of light, of joy…

But is she gazing into the chemist's window really, or standing before the rotary display stand outside the paper shop, watching? What tricks memory plays!

No, in front of the paper shop, rotating a rack of nasty postcards, is the young girl with the spotted beach ball in a yellow string bag who is seeking pictures for her collection of paper dolls.

? Who then, is this pregnant woman – what are her wishes.

? What are the wishes of the blonde woman, what does she seek.

Leaving the paper shop she pauses to slip into the plastic mac, then crosses the street directly from the kerb paying no attention to the constable on the zebra. Clutching the wad of cards her mind is now on the paper dolls laid out on the dining table, at home. She does not bounce the beach ball, which trails alongside to the right occasionally swinging into motion against her legs or the legs of passers-by. A blue impression refers the constable to the marginal sensation of some moments back now that her lithe movements are to be observed following a serpentine path through the traffic which again begins to condense for the roundabout behind him. Her willowy body is most clearly defined about the hips and buttocks where the fit of the mac is like a sheath, but the transparent material reveals too her slender waist, well-made breasts. She gains the pavement to the right of the two men, who have reappeared in the old position, one of whom – the one in the pale blue anorak – stares intently at her. The other takes no notice. In her hand as she goes by I notice the face on the postcard she has bought. It is the face of Christ, soapy, violently coloured, the conventional crown of thorns.

Bet this bitch just can't help lapping it up eh, just can't have enough.

What's biting you, Joss?

How?

Jumpy and razzled today, why?

Seen the card she had in her hand? Passionate type, I bet.

Same type as this, wan't it?

Out comes the novel from his pocket. On the card a bulbous blonde leaves a wood with a half nude man under a nasty sky clutching at her naked breasts. Its caption reads: RAIN STOPPED PLAY.

Make a smashing paper doll, she would, wouldn't she! No, the bitch in the mac, I mean.

? And the little troupe of cretins, whence their joy.

Their joy comes of bearing suffering in their bones; they do not need to seek it.

? And the pair of unhappy teenagers.

Are trying to find it they know not where…

What, suffering?

…because remember: reason does not replace emotion, but merely diverts it.

Thus spake Lho. Arise, Lho, take up thy myth and…

Lho! Laa…laa…la-de-daa…

Well, what's all that for?

Just laughing, Sean, dying with it: love… life, the lot, traalala. Remember Lawrence Henry, don't you, whose widow, you know… that's what we used to call him: Lho… something keeps coming… his babbling tongue. The human race simply loathes itself, he used to say. Facile, but not easy to discredit, not on the evidence, is it! Weeks it haunted me this, off and on, on and off. Then I wrote him a syllogism; but the post of course never got to the hut in the hills he used as a studio; it might be months. So I deliver it by hand: I am the human race. I love myself. The human race loves itself. September. Drizzling. Damp. Under this ash is Lho hanging by the neck. They say the corpse has an erection of the penis the moment the backbone snaps. Believe that, Sean?

Same's goats and donkeys; I've heard that before, yes, what's the point? You not losing your sleep over Lho, you just said?

Bloody shivering cold all of a sudden, you don't think? Christ what a life!

PREMIER FISHERIES.

It's just not true, you know, it's…

Finished?

The nasty postcard, scribbled all over, even across the legs of the discomfited lovers is still in my hand. He doesn't seem to mind my reading it: I have just rushed downstairs – the telephone rang, but it was the wrong number. Perhaps I haven't told you this before, but ever since I've known you I've had feelings and emotions I never knew existed. You've made a whole man out of me. I know real love, longings, needs, desires, and most of all, jealousy! Before, I must have been dead inside, I would never have wept over a woman leaving me. Is my life to go on endlessly/ Wanting you so much/I'll keep my love for you/Until the end of time/For I am truly happy/Knowing you are mine/The beauty of your body/And the passion that it holds/Delights me beyond reality/I am happy Dearest Lover/That you belong to me.

Then across the bottom: Darling *please don't take my life away,* heavily underscored.

He repeats pathetically, Y'know what a clean break means Joss? Quivering around the lips.

Wonder she hasn't left you before you bloody clot.

Again the unfocused crazed look enters his eyes. I feel he's going to bash me as in the corridor, at his last party, for unzipping his bitch's dress, but he hasn't the will: something's collapsed inside him. Without another word he turns, throws himself into the crowd, and off goes a red Mini-van cheekily accelerating from the zebra, nearside trafficator still winking from the roundabout at Pike Street. It continues winking until it snaps off abruptly in front of the library, the van building up acceleration to beat the lights, apparently, at Parry Road where, by the church and the fire station, a bus engine heaves heavily, lazily, inching, stopping, forward, stopping, until it breaks the line of the kerb disappearing before the eyes of the constable in a perspective that abruptly seeks new vanishing points at the triangular shape of Gwyddr Park. The constable observes the man in the mac leave his friend in the blue anorak, forcefully penetrate the crowd and walk a few paces before stopping at the lamp post outside Marks and Spencers to toss a blue paper ball into the green waste bin attached there, when with a muffled *crumph* the Mini-van rips into a car carelessly leaving the kerb. Sean's shaggy head pauses briefly over the waste bin. The hubbub of Sweeley Street dies down. Sean moves on. Far away a scream goes up. A blue Ford can be seen obliquely rammed into the Mini-van. A scream of pain. The driver is flattened against the seat. The constable wrenches at the crumpled door, which does not give. Everything has stopped. People move in jerks and glimpses. The constable pivots, guarding the zebra, watching the crowd interweave, overspill, swamp the island; the sound of their footsteps is like muffled hammerblows; like a distant sea a soughing, a scream. He screams. Stops. It starts again. Then stops. The front wheels of the van hang in the air, still spinning; people have accumulated: blobs, masses. Feet move abruptly. The driver of the Ford is ignored, shivering violently in the sun, unaware of the hole in his face. Their eyes connect like bolts; in the Mini-van the youth in the khaki smock grits his teeth as on a bit, drumming against the door, eyes on the constable who now looks towards the hill at the statue, beyond him, in the centre of the roundabout, of the great Welshman, 1856-1924, who martyred himself for the planting of Christianity in Darkest Africa. *Mewn Hedd!* The constable is aware of the impatient face of the youth framed in the window of the van whose nearside trafficators are winking still from the roundabout at Pike Street. But the pregnant woman must clear the second half of the zebra before the traffic is released. He ignores the youth. It screams again, spasmic, a force of nature. The constable keeps his mind on the door of the van, which finally yields to crowbar and axe. Another sonic boom rocks Sweeley Street, unheard; the aural field has contracted to a diameter of a few feet. At roof level seagulls screech *kee-oh kee-oh.* A seagull drops out of the sky. Two more. Three more. I can't speak while Titch deliberately watches seagulls dropping out of the sky. Three more, a lot, a cloud of seagulls suddenly roofing the courtyard, pecking at the concrete all over the place, deafly, Titch watching. More – a sea of seagulls. What's there in the concrete? They splinter the light, bobbing and weaving, bowing and scraping, beaks like brass bullets. Cambridge-blue delivery van loaded in the sun – Banks Press, Job Printers, Photo Engravers, Commercial Designers, *The Cambrian Weekly Record* – white on blue, stacks of crates, canyonned backyard, murals of ancient plaster, rotting brickwork, dusty window panes behind one of which, thrown open to the summer air, Tom is on the phone – *his* new red telephone: Yes, sure, what else, the chap dead?

His relatives are being sought.

The wreckage – cleaned the mess up yet?

It screams again. Then stops. They handle him; each smallest movement hurts so that for his sake – the UDC ambulance jangles up Pike Street from the direction of the West Shore: a white Humber with gold lettering, blue beacon. Following the roundabout it appears for a moment to be disappearing up the hill, but this is not so, it circles; the headlamps face Sweeley

Street, ribbed, glinting – for his sake they handle the disjointed bones, the mutilated flesh, indirectly, by means of the khaki smock – a sackful of quivering fragments. Traffic lights change. Nothing moves – the chimes have ceased – except the ambulance which now crawls to a stop. Then on a livid note the scream dies.

Had it, I'd say; kaput, finished.

The young girl with the beach ball observes blood froth and spread over the man's chest, spangled with broken glass, the eyeball of the other hanging by a grey thread down his cheek from a pulpy hole under the brow. Then the constable is on the pavement walking – a rolling heavy gait from the hips, looking down – towards his island. I follow him. Then I tear Sean's postcard up and drop the four equal fragments into the waste bin on the lamp post outside Marks and Spencers. Sean's balled-up blue notepaper is in my hand as I cross the pregnant woman crossing the zebra, whose back moves away in the butcher's window as the distance opens between us. Most striking is the ease with which her full body impresses itself upon the smock, now mauve, now pink, now pink and white, from the contour of her thighs as the wind moulds the material around them while I cross her crossing the zebra, to the brooding curvature of her back across the shoulders, the slope of her shoulders, the high position of her breasts, which are rather wide apart. There the constable is on his island, jewelled, bending towards this pregnant woman listening, and together they look at me, but not for long since the constable merely grins and the woman waddles on. And is the constable looking up the hill?

SNACKS.

9.47–9.49

Only in the ensuing void an interval as it were following upon the tumult could the voice was it a voice be heard again again wavering flickering on the aural threshold ashen rasping like the sound of raindrops on a forest floor. There was the darkness the sourceless vibration the immaterial suspension the distance. The leaden mass of tongue the protest the struggle to get back. He was toiling with this nescience inside a body which was without position in a vertiginous mad darkness without substance or limit: an infinite accumulation concentration dispersal to no end no purpose. There was a timeless waiting, on-going, motion and this motion was nothing, without source or centre, pregnant though with radiance possessing no measure – for with what would he measure. He was a dimensionless nothingness filled with sound and this sound was a space which commenced gradually to differentiate into intensities into measureless shapes and shadows, monochromatic, moving, where was an elated throbbing a waiting an interior awaiting its exterior its skin its evidence: waiting to get back where was a tumult. But there was distance.

Then being achieved a feeling.

But what was this feeling embedded in a struggling, a yearning? Even though monochromatic and attenuated the movement was a movement of men. There was at last a He, a They. They swam before him, uncertain vestments, grey intensities of unstable mass and contour hovering on the visual threshold so that it was impossible to establish for certain that these were not mere spots dancing and swimming there; whether their motion was voluntary yes or no, free or obstructed, for they appeared to coalesce to separate to penetrate one another with the greatest ease in a motion which with haphazard inevitability took them forwards backwards sideways it didn't seem to matter for there they remained never altering subject only to continual flux, endless interpenetration. They seemed to be getting nowhere. From every perspective the picture remained the same seemingly, a carnival as it were, clamorous concentrated engrossed directionless. And should one by chance lose his measureless path in the stamping maze all would vibrate with such voice of feeling not so appealing to his instincts, not imperious, solicitous rather, with a certainty. And should he not for instance heed or hear they stamped upon his head and ground it in the dust, sawdust, for in between the booths the maze was sawdust, velvety, stifling, pungent where the blonde girl splinters a heart, crouched. The gun crooked in her shoulder points towards this splintered heart but there, indisputably, is the smile on his face. She fires. He tumbles, simultaneously leaps up flickering, facing her, woodenly smiling. The cross impinges on the centre of the second heart. She fires. Beneath the cross he reels, spinning, leaps up woodenly dancing. She shifts the sights: three four five, knocks those down. Eight nine ten little wooden men. Beyond the cross she knocks the row to hell. Then back again. Nine eight seven, et cetera. Then the last. She raises the sights, knocks him over. He reels, leaps, dances spinning. Then all the hearts are splintered. Seagulls carve wild lines in the air, suddenly curved. The Big Wheel moves, stops. Legs dangle against the sky, stop. There are no seagulls. The Big Wheel moves. A young girl shrieks. It stops. The cross impinges on a bleeding heart. She wins a cuddly monkey black and white, three goldfish in a polythene bag, a card of pins, a pair of scissors. A man in a painted tent gives her a cut-throat razor, peering into her bosom. The music advances recedes vanishes following the migrant wind so that one is by turns centre or edge or limit of this sound, not sure. But inside the booths despite the tumult it is always for some reason dominant. There is a pause suddenly in this tumult as though everyone were simultaneously brought up short, thinking. But such a pause one notices only after the hubbub has returned to normal, just as the hubbub is most fully there only when true silence supervenes. And should one weary or unwary raise a voice a hand (of prophesy, of protest) they advance in advance of utterance, of gesture – for they are vigilant, armoured – in instant strange rebuke, unanimous. It is like that. They. Thankfully chanting hymns of joy. They doff their winding-sheets and wind down to the rocky stream down the whistling hillsides dotted with lambs, little lambs who made thee, thistle, gorse, broom – it is like that on the plains of Ysbyty-Ifan – tearing them apart. They are like that oh yes on cold and frosty mornings especially. They bring warmth, comfort, howling the while, the phalanx. And when in the crystal they find him on his rock basking or scratching listening to the musical little pebbles they drag him by the balls and run him screaming hair streaming up the hill, up, loosening boulders that crash and tumble and split his sides, yet to the end he does not seem to die. And why should he anyway and for whose sake. Like the dream he screamed each night way back as a boy. No, but in those days they were more human, more intolerant, you knew where you were, where you stood anyway – under his heel. And sometimes you could ease yourself into such a stance as eased the grinding, the pain, this was sometimes possible, all then left being his gross net weight, only that, nothing to complain about all in all you'd gained an accommodation and that was something. Something of value, no mean achievement; nobody could be ashamed of taking pity on the man calling him the while the underdog with a twitch of the nostrils, no. The good old days ah yes.

Prices of progress, can't have y'cake and eat it too, stands t'reason. He has a lilac face, this one, a paper rose. He says: What I call counting the cost, if y'get my meaning. Calculated risk – the slaughter on the roads. It's what I call this human race, everybody going hell for leather see. Where the hell's everybody running to – what's the fucking prize?

But along Sweeley Street no one is chastened by the tragedy; it will happen again. There are the usual unpremeditated crossings, recrossings, unaccountable changes of direction, spurts, pauses and directionless drifts that mark the holiday crowd on any day of the season in each successive summer. But for the report brought in by the traffic police there is nothing – not even in the behaviour of persons along the street – to suggest to the new constable that a fatal accident has occurred there earlier.

Has the accident though been fatal?

This new constable, asked, cannot with truth or certainty or even with interest, answer, being one step removed as it were from the event.

Then sometimes he would stop astonished, not astonished shaken to the roots, no rocked to the core so that all the little hairs stood on his cervical bones like the hackles of a brute rising, at the evil in someone's face; not so much the evil but to think that they could get away with it, such people, a face like that stuck under everybody's noses daily unsuspected, man or woman, yes women too. He would follow such a face around aghast, courting it so to speak, to speak; days, unobserved. And sure as day one day he would turn on you, literally, by the library say, the ironmongers, anywhere, not with, as you would expect: They've got It too, the bloody yellow swine! or a nasty word about the Vietcong, anythingsuch. No, plunging like a light into your puzzled eyes he'd gasp pleasurably, courting: Aaaah! Like a whore sucking you into the cunt the while. And what the hell good could flight do in any such contingency. Clobbering headbowed along the pavement he notes his weak-knees flicking ever forward, courteously giving way one to the other, turn by turn, the downtrodden shoe tips coming up for air, gasping, beholden, between footfall and footfall, rhythmically shuffling, small rhythms, joyless, unspringing through the violent spring, the green of summer, the lead of winter, the same. Always the same, old Lho, they'd say. Said Joss: Best designer west of the border though. Buttoning up his flies and there you are. Nobody called him ever anything more than that. And what if the cause of suffering be ignoble, it purifies just the same, granted no resistance from the vessel, this being one thing it will certainly not brook – resistance; it permeates and leaves the vessel to better days, brighter days, with no gratuitous residue of faith or fortitude and such, and the best must be made of that life being, as it is everywhere acknowledged to be, far from simple. So from suffering he clobbered on to temptation. The Temptation – called one though threefold – all inside the vessel, no agent, inside a man beside himself with hunger, it is as simple as that the first one anyway, the other two defining responsibility, the equation of power with evil, respectively. So clobbering on he got back to evil, how it should choose a vessel so perfect, so well adapted to its ends, bypassing all the animal kingdom: the evil that can stare you boltstraight only from the human face. Not that the animal kingdom altogether lacks its little ways; how could it! But what are they compared with the real McKoy. Nothing. He came upon Joss watching two donkeys copulate. In the sand, in the Red Sea, the Red Sea region where they knew each other first, the two, not the asses – the asses never knew each other, as it happened, however they tried – in the war. Not that they were too stupid to manage even that, they weren't, they were too clever by half as the saying is, the mare kicking, protesting, wilfully provoking as females tend to do, in the meantime so stimulating the stud that soon despite his power, poor chap, he could no longer bear it, couldn't summon the staff with stable effect, which hung between them like a flashing bolt while they slobbered, threshing and doddering across the wind-swept waste crazed, past desire.

He was mean old Lho. The little dodges he would stoop to to save a copper. Yet he would always be hard-up, Bid saw; he never would keep her but she married him just the same. What's called true love. His aristocratic manner. Which didn't run smoothly, naturally: two indigent coppers rubbed together soon wear each other out. He wore her out. She bore him on. He bored her eventually, artist or not. Famous insights apart, he stayed mean, clobbering from want to worry, worry to want, hard on her they said, her fresh young life. Best designer west of the border though, they said, sparing him not a thought. And why should they – his donkey's face, frayed tweed jacket leather-bound wrist and elbow winter and summer, his clobbering intensity; it was Bid they pitied only, in the manner of things, from the start. Two indigent coppers rubbed together could fail to bring out each other's shine – the shine of suffering – wasting their substance away, their best years, people remarked, reproachfully. People will be concerned one way or another as it happens, blissfully refining their misconceptions. But just the same they suffered, how could that be helped granted the sentient vessels they were, sensitive. They drove each other up the bitter wall with love, youth you know, floundering from discovery to discovery, always shocked anew in the way of the young, renewing their tattered vows. They lived with Mat, her sister – with themselves they couldn't afford to live, how could they – paying a small rent perhaps. No, they paid no rent, the house being theirs, Bid's and Mat's, left them by their Pa with wood rot and damp and chancy plumbing. Breathed onto them by this dead Pa God rest his soul, *Mewn Hedd!* They paid their way, they did not live on charity therefore, altogether. He was mean, indifferent to affluence. Oh yes and proud, so they said, with death in his donkey's eyes. For merited by intense great work death would come young, he saw, as to such as Seurat, van Gogh, with whom for him ended the history of European art. As he was wont to say: European painting simply cannot survive this displacement of chiaroscuro by pure chromatics, chiaroscuro being the very essence of our northern vision. Soon we shall come to tinted vapours and suchlike, then what! Too, he fancied he looked like Seurat, aristocratic suffering, fine eyes withdrawn. But he was a designer merely, they saw, with their usual warped acuity, best thing west of the border, true. A brave young death then, then Joss in remorse would be driven to his biography; for who did not know that Joss by now had borne poor Bid to bed, there comforting her fresh youth with all he had. All he had – that's saying something, poor Bid: the devil and the deep; Lho was deep all right, plodding hours, days, weeks over Croat's Soaps, Lamb's Margarine, with insight suitable for the Sistine Chapel no, the Mona Lisa, Minerva, for strangely it was women always, the problem; say Minerva – Botticelli he loved, for whom, when Bid conceived, he would call his daughter Sandra. When Bid did conceive though, whose child was it, people asked, concerned. They worked out constancies, recurrences, probabilities, arrived at fair conclusions. They. Back again where he began. To They. It was awful. Yet he wished to get back to them who in some moment of remote awareness he had left, their support and succour, the staff of life. But what had he to offer. He had tried, God knows, with his little talents, his little visions of grace and beauty. But what was wanting, as Bid complained always, was it not love. Ah, love; only a stone he had, a cave maybe, a stone that could have been filled and wasn't but with suffering. He called her darling and walked her along the prom and shopped her out Saturdays after lunch – Joss made him work mornings even Saturdays, but he loved her beauty only: he loved beauty, the innocent clot, it divided him from them, their comfort and laughter, their fun and games, and when death came young he was uncomprehending, as always, alone. How could he rest in peace then. Joss he called the Guv, like all the other men, common louts on the press floor, in awe. Not respect but fear: of this equation of power with evil which he saw in the Third Temptation. How could people talk of *the* Temptation as though it were one not threefold, the third far the most terrible. Hunger, the first, anybody could understand, it was only human; and He was human, hungry. You don't fast forty days and forty nights in a wilderness and not come to see your little visions of bread in stone, et cetera. He had seen Arabs do it, in the Red Sea region – thirty days and thirty nights – and so had Joss, and not that they didn't spend the thirty nights gorging either, they'd go all mad and visionary halfway through and could see bread in pure wind by the end of it. You've got to know your wilderness to under-stand its crown of thorns clawing the sky and its bitter wind searching like knives beneath the skin. The wilderness is no joke even on a contented stomach, its high and rocky wastes from which, if you are human, and was He not, you can't resist the wish to cast yourself down now and then the way temptation comes to persons on the Eiffel tower, it comes. With visions of the rescue of angels. Naturally. But to the human god it becomes a respon-sibility does it not to abjure the divine miracle, to accept the limitations of the flesh? No, the first two phases of the mysterious cycle, these are explicable, simple even, addressed to a god bent only on being human. But the third: Power? Whence is it offered or conferred, who the agent? – a concept different entirely from the other two, terrible in divine implication: a true temptation, profoundly horrifying, a proposition without the conditional, a bargain direct. So he clobbered to the inescapable conclusion that power and evil are one – and divine. Yet he abjured it, feared it wherever he found it, in Joss or anyone. Thus at the press easily he became Banks' prey and unprotesting property, upstairs in the little studio labouring over labels, the spangled literature of the seaside, church notices, gazettes for the Local Council. He gave all. And as though his humility required ultimate confirmation, the recommended turning of the other cheek, he was called upon too to give his Bid. Not even called upon: found that with no reservations in the matter he had long given her or that she had already given herself whichever you prefer.

How?

Joss had his dark bachelor's charm of course, his direct driving will, oh yes; but so had Lho his high white forehead, speculative mind. They were an equal match, about, making one whole or utter man; difficult for Bid, poor girl. Here we go – the usual sordid mess, Bid hot from one embrace into the other, but need it be described again? With the first rude shock – let's stop calling him Lho, Bid's name for him, adopted by Joss, *his* name for himself to get down to the truth of the thing – he broke all the glass in the flat, battering with futile fists against them. It was a red-hot case, mid-morning when all the world was grinding with varying degrees of satisfaction to one goal or another. No, all this is too commonplace what's so unusual about it. They needn't have been interrupted either but for Bid's anguished cries from the kitchen floor, for like all such cases they commenced, even though hot and hasty, with due respect for the marital bed. Strange connections! He broke the windows. The second time he broke the crockery. There was hell to pay, from Mat, her sister, who all but broke his head that time. He desisted, after that, frail spirit, from breaking anything. Except, slowly, his heart. But this took years, the thing being destined for a long and fertile life. Now Bid. She was unhappy; unable to find her own mind she would scream helplessly against them turn by turn, Joss, Mat, Lawrence Henry himself, but with what avail. Lawrence Henry summoned Joss to the prom one winter's afternoon, walked him silent out the rocks mossbound in the tide at the foot of Trwyn Bach – there are no rocks at the foot of Trwyn Mawr or that would have been more fitting, more impressive. Even so it was a fine grey setting for high tragedy, for action or ultimata to say the least. Joss is silent too, grave, as who would not be, granted the circumstances and the setting, monstrous in the heavily padded shoulders of the overcoats of the day, demob suit. They picked their way out to sea, slipping, clambering over the wet rock much as they had done years back on the inselbergs of the Red Sea, a big man and a smallish, in the war. So man to man they argued the toss. By timid processes then Lawrence Henry arrived at this: Well, can't you be just friends, without it coming to *that*? Said Joss, indignant: Never! That was the end of that. They talked on the way back in sickening mists about the press, the paper quota; things were looking up. Lawrence Henry would have more and more work on his hands, longer and longer hours. Very well then. Gradually Lawrence Henry eased himself into such a stance as eased in turn the pain, the only thing left being the gross weight of Joss on his mind which, in the circumstances, seemed little to complain about. Not so much as pitied from any quarter he went his way meditating from time to time on the mystery of the Third Temptation. Then he thought he might murder Joss: how else deal with ultimate power, evil absolute and divine. But would that win him back the love of a wife whom he had not lost, quite? Bid loved him, this was not in question, honoured his small demands, answered his preoccupied passions, preoccupied. All was not well but they hit it off, in a manner of speaking, about as successfully as other marriages up and down the street, not that there were many for comparison there, Sweeley Street being the business centre of the town. The condition of marriage can stand a lot however and survive, as he came to learn from the lot of several sterling couples in the neighbourhood, good solid people. His marriage was surviving; what would be the point of killing Joss. He killed himself.

Not so fast. He didn't do this right away, he took his time. In marriage circumstances rarely offer alternatives so extreme that the ultimate needs to be attempted in haste, marriage being more subtle than that, as also he came to learn. Oh he learned slowly step by step, clobbering from insight to insight; in the end he could have been a wise man, who knows, a bit the worse for wear perhaps. He came to look awful, quite eaten away or wasted as it is usually put, but then compared with the stringy young man with the large donkey's eyes who had become a soldier a few years back for want only of the will to resist, and groaned and grumbled his service out in the unrewarding wilderness, who was to say. He died young, though he had never truly speaking been young. But he isn't dead yet, death isn't all that easy, not by a long chalk, though people had begun to talk about him as a dead man long before he was known to be dead, especially in regard to Bid he was considered dead; for all his involvement in life he was, to all intents and purposes, truly dead. What did he give or take. Nothing. That's how he ended up. Long walks alone on bleak afternoons, along the prom or through the woods. Silent beautiful walks, presumably. Then in the woods he found his hut, the hut, a turning point, a coming full circle seemingly, a return to self, the ultimate confrontation. Here he capered with self like a toddler with a shadow; he was no more than this in many ways – a toddler in life as you might say, in the ways of the world, poor chap. Not that he did much to the hut at first beside sit therein, hours, damp, alone. Then he brought the stove, Bid took no notice, then his paints; she didn't care; then the bed. Not turn a hair. But all this took months, years maybe, the memory plays ghastly tricks even to one acquainted with the facts. He might have taken a sudden decision and gone bag-straight to his destiny in one fell swoop who knows, but this seems unlikely inherently to one familiar with the nature of the man; more characteristically he would have done it stage by stage, as though not doing it at all, unobserved, even by himself.

How did he come by this hut in the woods? By walking a bit farther than usual one Sunday morning. It stood by a stream he'd never seen just there; he'd seen it elsewhere he soon came to realise. Stone. Little musical stones to listen to for hours. In season he'd catch trout. He tried, that is, talking to those who did. Up at the farm to which it belonged he drank skim milk with a couple of the seventeenth century, felt very Welsh with them, their furniture, their bric-a-brac, their language. Bid had all but lost her language in long and alien communion with Joss. He left with large resolves to repair his loss, he was so very Welsh, he found. How though did he pay for this hut? Pittance from his weekly pittance; simple folk, grateful for small mites, small mercies. The view of the hills. It was ravishing; with a small extra walk, vast communions, solitudes, fusions of space, mist, clouds, valleys all purple and ineffable. He became so very Welsh, incomprehensible consequently to his countrymen. It was observed by them that he had taken a turning in life of a nature that was impressive and an affront both at once. He was not now so much unapproachable as unapproached. They came to. Back to They. He tired of seeking among this They, himself, his continuing, his evidence, his justification. Everything cannot be said, whoever the agent, whatever the view, all is relative, untrustworthy. He tired of them. He trod a path in the circumambient tumult towards the church.

Titch is in the press room now, Tom says, Ask him.

Tom is on the phone, *his* bright red telephone, taking a report. The youth in the Mini-van is sure to be dead by the next issue, for already in the basement they are running the week's *Record* on the old Dawson that's been there a year and a day, ever since the press first went up.

Being deaf Titch needs to use his eyes, but this he does only when it pleases him. Just now he doesn't care to; doesn't look up. He trims a block on the router, he braces the bench, guides the plate, watches the lead strip in coils. Along one wall of the press room, in the corner near which a door opens onto the closet where linotype slugs are melted down, are the two Heidelbergs which Titch has brought in since my day; in the centre of the room an American flatbed, also new. One of the Heidelbergs makes a kissing sound, the other is silent. Over his head the tired wartime slogan: *Miracles we perform instantly; the impossible may take a shade longer.* The router is new. It stops, then starts, stops. Titch switches the light off, examines the plate by an open window, nostrils twitching. Titch is nervous. Jumps and bites. Mousey, pink, nearly bald, grey, scrutinising the plate. No human in the world can better a job of Titch's, it is claimed. Far's human judgment goes, he would say, far's it's humanly possible, he would boast, displaying against the light the perfect register of type on the two faces of a printed page. Because of which it might well be true that Titch could run cigarette paper through one of his flatbeds and make no reverse impression; it might be true too that there is a micrometer in Titch's brain, for the machine does seem to complete itself in such a mind.

One of the fifteen men in the press room is heard to shout: It'll go back down, just push it, it'll go back down. But there is no acknowledgment; everyone continues as before, in an attitude of engagement. The machine clatter is great: several separate rhythms merging into one complicated grand rhythm whose elements it is easy to unravel. The foundation noise of this commotion is easily that of the colossal Dawson coming from the basement room – there is no basement, properly speaking, only a cubicle towards the front of the building, below the reception office – where are installed the Dawson, the folding machine, an electric guillotine, a paper-rack, a fire extinguisher. As there are no windows there the entire volume of sound from these machines issues up the short flight of steps to join the general hubbub of the press floor.

Even within the limited area of the press room the aural frame is not saturated: it is possible to become aware of the addition of a new noise or the cessation of an old. A machine being inked up runs a few moments then stops as the film of ink is tested for distribution. These irregular noises are difficult to ignore until the machine's normal rhythm takes its place within the complex rhythm of the press floor.

But the effect of the aural frame can be modified by familiarity. In the minds of men who work day in day out with the machine clatter it virtually ceases to exist, becoming audible only when the day's work is over and the machines switched off. Then a compensating clatter, as does the after-image of a colour, supervenes to fill the vacuum of the unaccustomed silence, to maintain the auditory mechanism in tune for the stresses of another day. It is an adaptation or specialisation of the auditory organs which, to the layman perhaps, amounts to a relative deafness.

But Titch's deafness is not relative, it is absolute; the deafness of one who has suffered the blasts of war and has lived half a lifetime growing into the new condition. There has been no other effect, it would seem, apart from the psychological, but here positive conclusions cannot be formed with any confidence: one would need to have known Titch before the war, in his youth, in Poland, his country. No one does. Everyone has learnt though that Titch saves up his thoughts; saves them carefully, hour by hour, then suddenly squanders them: squashes you somewhere, anywhere, among the machines, any place except the darkroom where he cannot read your lips, conjuring reminiscence after hungry reminiscence, deaf to his own voice, deaf to the world, like his machines.

Along his eyeline, beyond the type-high wood block which now he examines against the light for warping, he picks up my gaze. And how y'goin' Joss?

What does he see? The ex-Guv running to jowls, slackening, sagging, needing a shave. For Titch is sharp, free of equivoque, one-celled, certain. It is certain that Joss is slipping to hell. How's things? How y'goin' Joss, how y'slippin'?

And how y'going, Titch?

He rejects that wood block, goes to the cupboard for another, tests that on a steel plate, sight and touch, with a jerk of the thumb sends it to be proofed. This is Titch's mask – a profile in low relief, coinlike; no one sees more. But Titch is no machine, no rabbit, does not jump and bite, is human, is noble, is a man, I do not know, he does not say, I do not take the responsibility of saying. Titch is a habit of mine because of which it can be claimed he is me, is anyone, any of us, and does not therefore really exist. It is sometimes claimed that Titch stopped living since the war, is making money, is marking time, I do not know. I would not go that far in any case.

Then Tom comes down. They talk on the far side of the steel bench which bisects the room and stops short of the door leading to the furnace room. Behind Titch and Tom two linotype machines, very old, possibly the earliest models made, only one of which is in use for the time being, the operator of the other being just now injured, away in hospital – a minor accident, burnt or scalded with molten lead, with secondary complications too, it would seem, no one is sure, such is to be expected in the day's rounds, some say one thing some another, no one is certain.

It is certain that the Old Guv is slipping, no one doubts this. On all sides the men treat him with a new tolerance, a new good humour free of the habitual rancour, the habitual fear. As in the old days they discuss, no doubt with interest and satisfaction, his unfortunate passion for Bid – Lho's wife – her beauty, Lho's fatal inadequacies, Lho's end, and so forth, and so on. But the men are discussing nothing. This one is swabbing an inking slab with a ball of cotton-waste, that is bent over a composing stick, another is inking up the proofing machine, yet another is plugging away at the linotype, all reasonably apart, all disinterested, taking no particular notice of the Old Guv. Some manage even to be unaware of his presence in the room.

For his part though, Titch does not affect to ignore the Old Guv. His manner is natural: Joss has gone. Nor would he have so much as thought of it, but for Tom. The event, could such a usual visit be thought to amount to that, has quite slipped his mind. Joss has dropped by, as often he had done, to limber his fingers with the composing stick or on the linotype keys, and has left or faded away. This is as much as Titch could say, if asked. Not asked he couldn't say so much as this, his mind is elsewhere: on the block, the job in hand, concrete.

But Joss has not gone, as anyone in the room can see. He is here, has been here some time, standing by the rack where the various fonts of type faces are stacked, indecisively turning this way and that, waiting apparently on someone, something, to make an interruption, profit by an interruption, biding his time, it might even be thought stooping to conquer, for has he been known to quibble ever over postures adapted to his ends? Never. Can be seen, through the press-room window, the grey hump of St John's, the wall, the cambridge-blue delivery van standing on its shadow in the courtyard. And then Tom leaves, boss-eyed, smirking, but stops on the other side of the steel bench, silhouetted, facing the Old Guv, different, very different, oblique, obliging. Now why should Tom be remote, embarrassed, obsequious, all at once? It might be that he cannot pity the fallen mighty (for to cast oneself down without fear is a test is it not of responsibility, power strengthened by choice of an alternative – thus, on the second of the temptations, spake Lho), that or any other of the complicated feelings naturally attendant upon stepping into another's shoes or inheriting the fruit of another's labour, Tom being conscientious to a fault, deferring, slyly disputatious just the same. Not to be avoided, one supposes, in one living with deaf old Ma all these years, and her violin, a Strad he says, which she makes him play for his supper, nightly after supper, willing her to will him the crumbling cottage in Gwyddr Terrace poor Tom. But the truth is this: it is beyond the power of any man to step into Joss' shoes he not consenting, even had these been abandoned along with the works, which of course they were not. The most fumbling creator is after all unique, made to his own measure, Tom could not but know. It is Joss therefore who seeming to reach down rather bellows: Awright Tom? Everything awright then?

And the Old Guv is once more there, how simple that was, as in the old days. No one present now doubts, or affects to doubt, even the deaf, hearing the old thunder, watching the old force burgeon in speech and aspect, that the Old Guv is here, in the flesh, bestriding the narrow works as of old, like a colossus. To a man, in various ways, there is a response, instant, pavlovian, though not in every case overt. In Titch's case, for instance, not, but what does that matter! Joss has been heard, even by the deaf.

The work is finished when form has attained its plenitude (thus spake Lho) and the creator defecting could be loyal still – to his purpose. Out of wisdom, call it, and not at all from any sense of defeat, though there might be those, blind to finer issues, who altogether fail to see the point. For the moment comes when taking on a life of its own the creature might be seen to shed its creator like the apprentice his sorcerer. Form once achieved cannot but persist, it being what it is.

Why then does Joss drop in, hang around, limbering his fingers, doing his unregarded stint on the linotype, breathing down Tom's neck upstairs, in the editorial? Does the question mean anything, really?

The creator might defect too, lacking any sensible alternative, in contempt for the creature of his making. Then what? Then they are bound just the same, one to the other, in that most despairing state of all love – faith – bound creature and creator and in spite of themselves by explicit though perhaps mutually unacknowledged links, impotent to sever the image of a relationship from its referent. So the question is this: Could Joss not, abandoning the works, free himself too? Is the man bound still even in his considered descent? No one knows. Or rather no one knows aright, for certain, and without forcing conclusions. Some say one thing, some another, all proposing reasons external to the situation, e.g. that Joss was discontent with his pile, that Lho was on his mind, that it was Bid, et cetera. People talk; talk and talk. Nobody can call his life his own, not in Caedmon.

Suddenly sold up his business and running to seed, they say, but harmless, quite harmless.

And the pregnant woman sees at once that the butcher has got something there. For the man drifting bright from the park to the rock, from the rock to the park, among the trappings of the seaside and season, the beach balls and beach things, the spots and stripes and chevrons, *is* running for all to see, to seed, though, despite the gossip, she knows nothing of his prior or his present states. Nobody knows much of his present or his prior states, but talk continues to be sure, speculation; for Joss is known, Banks Press is known, rather, to every tradesman in town, to every trades-man's wife, and of course to others: to shop assistants, for instance, and suchlike. Brummagen or something, they say, Londoner maybe, who knows! You don't chuck up a flourishing business like that for nothing at all, do you, not for nothing! People agree. Tradesmen, their wives, their shop assistants and customers, all Caedmon in a word, and part of the holiday trade as well: persons such as the pregnant woman in the pink, pink and white, or mauve smock, who is not a local but visiting, for a few days, her mother and aunt, also not locals, but residents of some years' favour. She has watched him loiter, he has loitered, is loitering, up Sweeley Street towards the park, down the street towards the rock, all the morning. As though trapped when, for diversion, he is equally free to climb the rock, to stroll the prom, laze on the beach, or light a bus for the West Shore (the Crafnant Pass is beautiful, wild, deserted) or simply extend his idle strolling, so feeling inclined, past the park, past the fair, past Maesdu and Llanwrog – the last villages on the plain – to the foot of Trwyn Bach where beyond a picturesque scatter of mossy rocks another blue bay opens, also desolate, Caedmon and District not lacking by any means in places of public privacy. But does he choose any of these available alternatives? Obviously no. For time passes and he wanders, though perhaps plagued by indecision – for once he was observed to have boarded a bus, a number Eleven, Groesffordd, then abruptly, on the running board, to have changed his mind, charge, neck craning, along the pavement in the direction of St John's, stop, think apparently for some moments, then to turn in his tracks and head again towards the rock, tramping the pavements now this one now the other as the morning shadows shorten and the sunlight sharpens, scrutinising shopfronts, studying passers-by, drifting. From the rock to the park, from the park to the rock.

Why?

Except to the pregnant woman idling the time away on the concave bench below the flower boxes on the roundabout the question is of no consequence to anyone. Not even to the constable who pivoting on his island cannot from time to time help observing the blue anorak now close at hand, now some distance away, interweaving with the crowd, sampling the pavements.

But all this was a long way back, long before her time. She was a schoolgirl, she remembers, when Joss Banks seduced the man's wife, one of his staff, a commercial artist; she was young, she hadn't been told, but she had heard. Then the man found out that the child wasn't his. And hanged himself in a wood. Then his wife married Joss Banks, then Joss Banks married this man's wife, something like that, the wife of this commercial artist. That's what the girl remembered with the cone of candy-floss hair. Then Joss Banks began going to seed, so the story goes. *That's* the story some say, bold spirits. But it is a story without point or purpose, without core or meaning, in regard to which it does not help to say: That's the way it is, For what it is worth, As gossip would have it, I cannot swear to it, and so forth. It doesn't warrant such attitudes. For who in any issue of disputed paternity even including for the sake of the argument the testament of the one known parent, the wife, can prove anything? And what man of sound mind would venture so far as to perpetrate on himself this act of supreme irresponsibility on such a known uncertainty? Where is the point? People talk. All one can do is listen. And one listens of course, one observes. But the impression, even on one who knows the facts, is oblique, in three-quarter view as it were. Such a view though, neither full face nor profile, has its advantages, combining as it does elements of the other two: as the agent sees itself, as the agent is seen, or even seen to be seen. Equidistant between two full-length mirrors in a shoe shop he sees himself multiplied two hundred and fifty-six perhaps or even five hundred and twelve times each way, front and back. In an instant he is back on the pavement, among substantial flesh and blood, quaking; for the paradoxical diminution of the creature in multiplication... much can be said of this. But catching his eye I mouth my request, and he falters, gestures me into the yard, through the damp little closet where linotype slugs are melted down in a primitive little furnace on the concrete floor. I nudge him in the waist. He turns about as usual without using his neck, preferring as he does always to confront things. I point out that the door hinge needs mending, that it has been that way years, that this is important. He agrees, doubtless resentful. Then I comment on the job in hand, the job on the Heidelberg, Lamb's Margarine. He says: Third colour running this morning. And lights a cigarette without offering the packet, it doesn't occur to him let's say, spews the first exhalation out, coughs, smoke shreds from his mouth, he turns away, tiny grey hairs sprout from his neckback, he coughs: Sorry, coughs again, then: Nice, isn't it! I mouth my frank opinion: It's stunting, it's *chi-chi*, and he answers – the inhalation seems to hurt for he closes an eye and whistles through thin lips while the lids of the other tremble and its pupil bores like a drill: Selling, Joss, selling. Then challenges: Anything wrong then? Being blind on design simply, not his cuppa – makes no bones about it either: Client's happy I'm happy, that's about the size of it! What else could he say, all considered? I say to him: Soon come to notice trends, you know, once you leave the trade. The style's dead, Festival-of-Britain, dead as ashes.

Alive and kicking then he faces substantial flesh and blood on the pavement, quaking. This crowd. Its motion. A motionless crowd – try to think of that! This motion has its terrors too, its instinct and inevitable duality, its ebb and flow, its to and fro, its future, its past, its on-going, its *uncertain choice.* Facing one way, flowing, going one way, a crowd is nothing, is direction merely, time streaming, a future, a procession (and where is there terror in a mere procession). But the to-wards and from-was, the on-going, the bombarding of the instant, the defying of the locus, this – he pivots, altering direction but not context – from the farthest perspectives, in unknown incurious eyes, the future advances blind, towards. Beyond his shoulder a future now turned past recedes, bearing an image. He pivots again: the first then advances, on his back. It sees, in the centre of the pavement, a middle-aged man staring down Sweeley Street as though waiting perhaps, as though vacant. But either way the instant is bombarded, the locus defined: the advancing eye forms an image, the diminishing back bears a memory. A crowd is not *it*, nor even *they*; but *I*. On this plane the diminution of the creature multiplies like decimal places to extinction. So he stands on the pavement, quaking, staring: he is a dot, he is a term in a disjunct series, he gazes at a rock.

He sits on the iron stairs leading to the first floor – store rooms, my old office, Lho's old studio – inhales again, bares his teeth, squints. I suggest that in the trade what we need is to keep one jump ahead sort of thing. Then a seagull drops out of the sky. He deliberately watches it. Two more, three more, dozens; dozens of seagulls suddenly pecking at the concrete courtyard all over the place. I can't speak while Titch deliberately watches seagulls dropping out of the sky. More, seas of seagulls splintering the light, bobbing and weaving, bowing and scraping, beaks like brass bullets, the cambridge-blue delivery van loaded in the sun, Tom on the phone: Sure, sure, got that – curve; that what you said before, in't it, c-u-r-v-e! C Charlie, U Uncle, R Robert, V Victor, E Edward, yes?

No. What Titch says is this: The man from the Ford refuses, doesn't refuse, does nothing. Nothing but stand mute staring through the hole in his face. It is clear that he is struck, as the saying goes, he is struck. Over and again he rises from the place on the pavement where he has been made to lie, and returns to the wreckage struck, staring, unaware of the eyeball dangling by its grey thread against his cheek. It is now known that this blue Ford swung out at a lick from the curve, the youth in the red Mini-van didn't stand a chance in hell, didn't know what hit him and just as well. Had it. Kaput. Finished. Before you could say Jack Rabbit.

Robinson you mean, old man, Jack Robinson.

Where's the feathers?

Rabbit!

I'm asking where's the others?

Only one; carted him off too.

Clean the mess up yet?

No. On Sweeley Street the wreckage has drawn a crowd from far and wide: from the beach, from the town, watching. The after-presence of the pathetic makes violence seem all the more terrible in retrospect; from the upper decks of buses persons arrested, impatient perhaps, gaze at its mute trace in the torn-up rutted-up road, in awe. Seagulls attracted by the commotion drop out of the sky. Onto roofs and fences, onto the blunt twin towers of St John's, into the courtyard of the printers behind the church where Tom's eyes are on the murals of rotting plaster, the ancient brickwork, dusty window-panes, rosettes, gargoyles, gable-ends, chimney-stacks, smoke (smoke in July), shadow, sun, clouds, sky, twin towers of St John's, aerials.

From the first floor Tom observes the two men talking: a khaki smock, a pale blue anorak.

Saying, you know, I remember as a boy. Two different kinds of men. Titch crushes the cigarette, flicks the stub-end off like a missile, rises, dusts his seat, finds Joss' eyes: Them with whips, and them with wounds.

All I'm trying to say is that these pastel effects've had their day, Titch, that's all I'm saying, these dots and circles –

And St John's, strangely, begins tolling. The seagulls explode, hang in the cage of canyon, legs trailing, shadows dappling the concrete. But Tom hears nothing, properly speaking; the words merge and tumble, offer alternatives of cognate sound: Tremble as a toy, tender as joy, remember a boy, ships and woods, whips and hoods – the noise of the seagulls is great, *kee-oh, kee-oh* – chips and woad; he only thinks he hears, inducing meaning, supplying context, his mind on the phone: Right! got that then, curve – came round the curve! Eyes on the concrete square, the fragment of iron stairway bracing the building, its lace-work shadow, two men, their shadows, the van, the crates; but what he sees is the crowd, the wreck, the constable, the telephone booth, the library, the ambulance, the constable, the van.

It bore a Conway trade name. The birds. They mushroom, cloud the canyon, resentful. Two dogs sidle in from the mews, locked, tails tangled. Titch laughs out loud; he doesn't hear their yelps of pain.

Joys of love! he mocks. Toys above, Boys of love. Ploys of Jove.

Reminds me, ever seen donkeys do it? Bloody funny. Down in the Red Sea you know. Hours and hours. Climate or something.

Know what he used to say about that one, old Larry, don't you! Good story that he used to say, if y'get the meaning.

Smiles deafly, samples deep, deeper than ever, searches my eyes for the weight of his dredging. Skilled in pain, feelings specialised: a murderee provoking the shriek that guides the murderer's blow. He says: Put on some weight, Joss, have you?

Haven't noticed, Titch, always been bit of a big boy like, ha'n't I? Pound or two maybe, here and there.

Pound or two round the chops alone, ha'n't you? Filling out, suits you too the new life, don't it

New life, new love, new laughter, ha!

What's all that for?

Just dying with laughter, Titch – life, love, the lot, the old story you know. When's a duck become a drake?

He looks incredulous, suspicious, doesn't answer. When's a duck become a drake, go on, riddle me riddle, I mean?

Doesn't know of course, not Titch.

When it circumnavigates the world, heard that one?

Doesn't laugh, and nor do I. Comes acid: Funny!

What y'nibbling at then now?

Happy, aren't you! Chaps go off the job, go to seed usually, don't they? Grow weeds. You keep fine, happy, keep an interest in the old firm, put on weight. Got loads left, ha'n't you, retiring early like. Like starting on another life all over again, I suppose?

Up and doing y'know, no use sitting around moping, is there?

Well the old firm can always do with you dropping in like this o'course, specially these days, short-handed you know, summer and that.

Keeps me on the go it does, don't mind admitting.

He says: I see! Cautious. Sees a lot, seen a lot old Titch, right here in this building, since way back. That's what's in his eyes.

Best designer west of the border you used to say Joss, wa'n't he old Larry?

Sure. Had taste, imagination, Lawrence Henry. Not much of what it takes though, did he?

Doesn't answer, thinks, drops his eyes, observes the stub end smouldering at Joss' feet: ghost of a spark furiously consuming nothing, embedded in ash. All gone to waste in't it! Was young to die like, wa'n't he!

Green ink on the khaki smock forms a face that grins. Seagulls swoop, pounding the concrete, dozens, flapping, *kee-oh, kee-oh*; canyon dizzy with them, Titch waiting: God rest his soul, eh Joss?

Ai, and put it in chains.

Don't hardly seem time ago, does it!

(*That's* what I mean – I was beginning to wonder, was it him or me or what – exploding, expiring, expanding, contracting, it couldn't be me, but if it wasn't then was it him or no or me at last I'm seeing things or something – there – sparkling, spinning, receding, ah really no, only stars setting in his crazy eyes.) But he was contemptuous of death you know, Titch, that's one thing he always used to go on, remember, about us crossing the bar, us Europeans – a lot of nonsense he used to say, there wasn't any bar to cross, the body goes empty to the grave, life's never lost, sort of, we keep inheriting it like, from the dead, inheriting it, so it goes on, or where does it keep coming from – indestructability of spirit you know, stuff this Welsh Martyr brought back from Africa; always was a great one for other people's convictions, old Lho, wasn't he.

That what his wife called him, eh – Lho?

Way he signed his designs, you known that all along –

That what you call him too?

What's in a name? – Lho, Larry, Lawrence Henry, same bloody fraud – what's in a name? He *was* a bloody fraud you know –

Whips and wounds, Joss, like I said. Look around you. Harder you slash, louder you shriek, in't it! Anything you wanted, by the way?

What's the tolling for? Gets on your nerves doesn't it – what's it all for?

What tolling?

He said. I said. He said. I said. Wearing me down, stars dancing in his crazy eyes.

Question of those old drawings – Lawrence Henry's you know – those old sketches upstairs, Croat's Soaps, nudes and things. Now we're married – me and Bid – be proper like if she keeps a hold on them, won't it?

You *want* them, Joss?

Yeh; private reasons you know how, she says for me to fetch them back, they're his. She wants his things.

He laughs – barks: That's right! Lights another cigarette, spews a dense cloud sideways off twisted lips, shreds tobacco – *pta*, *pta* – from his tongue, tosses the match, manner dangerous, clanging, bitter. Friend of Lho's, two the same: sufferers, sacrificers.

How about it, Titch?

Have t'be thinking about that, Joss, property of the firm and that, you know.

Like how?

Like I said.

Like you said like what?

Copyright and that – needs thinking about.

I'm out of the trade now, Titch; need them personally.

Not so fast, Joss, no need to shout.

His widow's property!

Your wife, you mean.

Got nothing on me conscience, Titch.

Never did much, did you?

None your bloody business, either.

Ahre, take it easy now, now then.

Bloody Polak swine you she you've had your rope, she's going to have them, won't she now!

Light-hard he kicks and threshes air, croaks, puny frame tugging writhes in the smock at first indignant, angry then, then frightened, so that the moment his toes regain the ground off he goes scrambling, scurrying. Back to the works, *his* works, *his* men, *his* atom, furious. But muffled by the tolling this voice insists: Not so fast Titch, now then! hot on his neck. On a patch of neck a cord leaps blue, a cord, a rope, a sheet stretched between desperate stresses, a thinking pain concealed. He yelps, claws at the broken door, the latch, the hinge, the testimony (and how often had he been shown this rotting thing, the rot, the rust, the riven plank crossed upon itself like forlorn cross, ghost, gibbet or stay). It gives. I peel the frantic fingers off. He screams. Stops. Kicks and bites. Screams. I straddle him, locked, force the mouthing face away. It dips towards the crucible, purple flesh and grey, metal covered with steam, with ash, so that the grey scum floating there is barely visible. Titch is strong, is difficult, jerks, slipping. But as the face enters the pungent fumes the scream changes, a gurgle, a sob perhaps, which instantly dies, struck dumb. Protest is violent through his frame – the spasmic shudder of life released from will. Smell of burning air, a sizzling brief drowned protest, garbled, from the throat, bereft, a slipping sound consenting. This flesh leaps in terror, like jabbering cat clawing covered suddenly with hands with nails rivets bolts turn of the screw, lugs irons arms voices bobcock bibcock stopcock shouting the while, *kee-oh kee-oh* a clamour a tumult, this closet, jostling shouting, proclaiming exclaiming exhuming. Lead stuck to this skin this face hardens silver like stars embedded there which here is grey there livid, raw, puckered, eyes there which staring nowhere everywhere, drained dumb past pain yet see the futile point in Joss' eyes, grey eyes questioning this inevitable tryst: *Why me?* Dumbly disintegrating he faints then in the tumult, knowing.

Why can't a man be left alone!

WHIPS AND WOUNDS.

10.20–10.21

A simple accident. So it seems to all the press, to all the men but Tom.

10.22–11.07

The sun clouds over, the light grey-green.

A helicopter drags itself into the air above the roofs of the hotels that hide the crown of Trwyn Mawr. The hotels do not hide the crown of Trwyn Mawr, except from that point at the head of Sweeley Street where the constable on his island pivots. From the other end of Sweeley Street, from Gwyddr Park for instance, it is the crown of Trwyn Mawr that is visible, not the hotels. Behind the geranium beds in the roundabout, behind the island where the constable pivots, the hotels now sink into a crowded perspective defined by the jagged roofline of the great shops. The obligatory locus for this view is the eye of the fountain which stands at the centre of the park. From this locus the toy figure of the constable stands on an exact line with the statue of the Welsh martyr by which he is dominated in the same proportions – three to two – as those in which the statue is dominated by the height of the rock. The slightest movement to the right or to the left of this locus destroys the symmetry of the view and causes the composite image to shift, inversely, to the left or to the right. Movement along the rib of Sweeley Street, likewise, while not disturbing the symmetrical orientation, as happens laterally, upsets relative proportions. So that at a given distance from the fountain and approaching the constable the constable achieves the height of the statue just as the statue achieves the height of the rock. At this point the crown of Trwyn Mawr commences to disappear beneath the line of hotels at its foot – a point between the library and the church of St John's opposite. There is nothing to mark this point along the rib of the street except, at the moment, a man with a lilac face standing there, but it is easy, though this is hidden from the immediate view, to realise that in the opposite direction the horizon has dropped in accordance with the movement of the locus up the slope of the hill. The Great Western Hotel no longer towers quite so commandingly in relation to its own view of Sweeley Street; the position of the locus – the man with the lilac face – is now on a level with its first-floor windows. At this level the top of the roof of Ross's Garage just becomes visible; roads radiating from the park form an actual rather than a conceptual star at whose heart the bronze bowl of the fountain is now unambiguously an ellipse. That position of the locus from which, along the rib of the street, the crowns of constable, statue and rock meet on the one hand, and the roof of Ross's Garage follows a straight line into the first floor of the Great Western on the other, is not strictly speaking at the centre of Sweeley Street but more towards its head, nearer the rounda-bout. This is due to the gradient, which is even and gentle. The slightest movement of the locus along the midrib of the street in either direction while disturbing this particular balance simulta-neously creates others. Thus in the direction which brings it within inches of the constable's feet the constable's head towers above that of the statue and the crown of the rock while in the opposite direction more of the roof of Ross's Garage becomes visible, and the locus now stands on a level with the second floor of the Great Western which in its turn is lower, nearer the horizon line.

Very gently then Sweeley Street slopes, and the movement of the locus up and down or across it creates images that vary from moment to moment and which sometimes even contradict one another according to the continuous comings and goings, the crossings and recrossings, the purposeful proceedings, intervals and pauses, or spontaneous changes of direction, of persons along it. Function apart, no image is therefore more meaningful than any other; no position of the locus is more significant than the next.

In the interior of St John's the image of Sweeley Street is severed from its referent. This image is supported however by the regular though uneven sound of traffic and by other noises. The locus is the centre of an aural frame whose radius is not great, its limits being the sound of breakers along the beach, the cry of seagulls overhead, the abrasive texture of activity along Sweeley Street itself. The visual field now is restricted to the interior dimensions of the church where from the left aisle exact perspectives lead the eye towards the altar and the complicated fenestration above it. But penetrating this precise visual field are images no less precise that refer to the wider aural frame. These from time to time impinge upon the visual field with such clarity as occasionally to destroy it so that the sound of a bus for instance decelerating for Parry Road produces an image that quite overpowers that of the altar and the saints above it: the relative section of Sweeley Street appears where these images should be, resulting in a surreal juxtaposition – half sacred, half profane – in which the clatter of footsteps on the pavement outside superimposes images of nylons, plimsolls, brogues, ice-cream cornets and holiday slacks upon those of the saints. The fourth wall is thus alternately concrete and immaterial; Sweeley Street discloses its images in simultaneous or contiguous association relative to the transforming function of the locus.

Sweeley Street projects itself too into the show windows that border it like so many dispassionate eyes on either side, into the shops in moving shadows and intensities of reflected light. Along the street the awnings are out so that each shop door is now hooded like a lens and thus more readily transmits images from the outside which continually move and play on the interior walls. Each shop is in this way an eye or camera or camera eye across the intimate face of whose retina or screen can be read, even though monochromatic and attenuated, something of the movement and clamour in constant play outside.

Thus the blonde with the blue plastic mac – at the moment no longer wearing the mac but carrying it in her white handbag – wandering aimlessly from the park to the rock, from the rock to the park, is the centre or source of a series of images produced in various depths and distances from herself, of herself, some of which she sees, others of which she does not. From the various show windows she is aware of a mirror image at times parallel, at times in inverse motion, to the direction in which she moves; at times familiar in proportion, at others so strangely compacted elongated in the generalised setting of the crowd surrounding her that she is obliged to stop and stare, full-face, profile, three-quarter face seeming to bear no relation to each other or to their common referent – herself. To these images the blonde girl of course adds the concept which explains them all – the context of the locus: I am in a street, for instance, I am in a shop, I am in a church staring at an orange-coloured flag over the rood screen. In a pew in the north aisle is a middle-aged man crouched in prayer gripping the pew rail ahead. The visible portion of his face reveals a large stubbly jaw, a whiskered ear, a few grey hairs. Tiny brown freckles dot the skin on the back of his hand. The legend on the picture postcard in my hand reads: *A copy of this famous painting is in St John's Church, Caedmon. If you watch the eyes closely they will suddenly open.*

Beneath the painting is a balled-up wad of blue notepaper which the girl picks up to dispose of later. She does not understand why anyone should litter a church, certainly no one of the demeanour and appearance of the gentleman in the blue anorak bent over the pew rail seemingly lost in prayer. For it is an irony of the moment that the man's posture, head resting on the rail between clenched fists, can be construed as one of devotion. There is no visible trace of the tremors at this moment running through his body, there is no evidence of any kind of distress, so the girl ceases to take notice and consults the purpose for which she has come, namely to investigate this notorious trick of the eyes of Jesus, this spasmic tic or flutter or godlike mockery universally claimed to answer to the inquirer's gaze. But on the postcard, whether because of the scale of the reproduction – or on account of the shiny surface of the print – or due perhaps to a divergence, particularly in the blues and reds, of the colour values from the original, noticeable though not remarkable, the miracle does not seem to occur. Under the closest scrutiny the eyes of Jesus do not open. They remain closed, so far as she could see, to the world, though conceivably they might equally well be open staring at a point on the flagstones a few feet away – the posture of his head permits of either interpretation. Above the collar of the man's anorak thin reddish wrinkles are stretched across his neck like threads of blood. Threads of blood trickling down the forehead stop short above the shuttered eyes of Jesus. The lashes, long, darkened as though with mascara cast a faint crescent of shadow onto each cheek, deepening the Man-of-Sorrows expression, suggesting a remembered pain, a remembered joy, remembered pain.

He died ages ago, the pregnant woman informs her husband.

Pivoting, the constable takes in the couple with a glance.

Crushed to pulp inside the van, y'never heard such screams. Before they got him out he was dead; pulling out from the kerb you know.

Round the curve, you mean, curve.

No, kerb, don't you tell me what I mean. Down by the church. I watched him. All in a flash, *crumph!* like that. Bits and pieces.

Still no one can say with confidence whether the man is dead, yes or no. Beneath the overloaded colour of the shops, in the pageant of holiday-makers, it remains the news of the moment: an undertow of nausea running through the restless tides of Sweeley Street. No one acknowledging it or not is unaffected by the memory, even those who happen upon the scene long after the wreckage has been cleared and the blood and oil covered with sand. The eye witnesses have departed, spreading the story through and about the town; but the shopkeepers, they who labour in the street throughout the year, retain the after-presence of tragedy with occupational care and thoroughness. It has settled like an unwholesome odour into the memory and fabric of the day. It is they principally who keep alive the horror of the morning, defying the imprecision of human recollection, trading it with the colourful trifles of the seaside and season – the beach balls and beach things, the rude postcards, the brilliant plastics in spots and stripes and what-not, relating, repeating, transmitting. Some persons are more impressed than are others: the teenage couple in oilskin jackets, for instance, hardly at all. The *Valetta* – grained, marbled, panelled, bambooed, mosaicked – is crowded. The girl says to the youth: Let's go somewhere. The youth does not answer. Close behind him a woman is explaining: No, what I think about that picture is that you could make Him look if you want to: any sinner, any man, anybody. He could open His eyes only by you wanting Him; He's as good as blind otherwise. More than that, when He does open His eyes it's for you alone; the next person doesn't count at all except he tries for himself. Then never mind how many of you, each man gets his own look-in, see, private-like if he wants it, from Christ.

But the husband of this woman – she wears a pink and white smock over a pregnant figure – is gazing at the wall, opposite the door, where could be observed silhouettes vaguely projected there from the pageant outside, along the pavement. Curiously, the images move inversely to the direction of motion of their referents, and upside down. He turns from time to time to refer some image to its source on the pavement outside. Persons going by are unaware of course of the record of their passage projected on the inner wall of the coffee bar; their actual movements caught in discrete flashes construct a meaningless geometry: a stride arrested Egyptian-wise between footfall and footfall, the incomprehensible twist of a torso, a face turned skywards, a child stooping; the visual field alters continually in depth from the movement of traffic across it. Now a bus stops so close to the kerb that fragments of the shop façade are reflected in its windows among the passengers. Fragments, since only those sections of a given window which stand against the dark interior of the bus can reflect anything. In other sections the gaze penetrates the width of the bus beyond which it is blocked, on the far side of the road, by the row of buildings in shimmering sunlight there. Relative to the dimensions of the bus window these buildings appear minute – three or four to the width of each window which, at a guess, could be no more than say, thirty inches across or so. Which suggests that on this perspective plane the width of each building is virtually no greater than seven and a half to ten inches – a measure which might be established with even greater precision simply by marking these distances off, with a suitable instrument, in the green paintwork of the window frame. Yet even on this miniature scale the awning over the shop at the centre of the window, measuring no more than seven inches say, by four, can clearly be read: MORGAN'S THE PHOTOGRAPHIC CHEMISTS. Against the glare the heads of persons in the bus appear dark, featureless. Substantially though the visual field is limited now to the width of the pavement. Along the corridor thus formed figures cross each other in either direction, edging, dodging, interweaving, colliding. Lips open and close, smirk, curl; shoes strike the pavement soundless for the tumult of Sweeley Street at large drowns all but the most immediate noises. The bus too though stationary has not ceased in its mechanical throbbing. But then it pulls out, the reflections vanish, the patternless depth of Sweeley Street is pushed back to the limit of shopfronts on the opposite pavement beyond which, in the line of show windows under the awnings can be seen the long-haired figures of a youth and a girl, both in oilskin jackets, leaving the entrance to the coffee bar. As they pass close by the husband of the pregnant woman the girl is heard to say: Where we going now then – it's such a brilliant day!

This can hardly be argued, even in the sacerdotal gloom of St John's. In the murky light falling from the rose window onto the dully polished pews Sean's blue notepaper seems almost white; the pallid stained glass has subtracted the hue, almost the substance, from my hand. Textured into negative and positive creases, no shadows mark the wrinkles of my palm or those of the notepaper. The interior of the church is shadowless, as is to be expected from the filtering effect, along the four sides of the building, of the windows. The rose window is smaller than those over the chancel, to counteract which the glass is paler. The aisle windows being larger, are set in a greater thickness of wall than are the clerestory windows. They are also of a denser colour and texture.

I see at once the case for a sacerdotal light which dematerialises, purifies, severs spirit from substance, image from referent. In this lightfall all matter is deformed.

My tremors become so acute before they finally cease that I am obliged, by way of containing them, to get hold of the pew rail ahead. It occurs to me that these tremors might be the result of hunger, of cold, but to this, while they last, I cannot give a thought. Vaguely though I promise to take stock of my condition at some later time, to report to myself as it were, on the state of my well being. In the meantime there is the convulsive twitching, the dumb jabbering, the flesh to all intents and purposes out of control. So violent these convulsions soon become that after a bit my teeth refuse to remain clenched. It is as much as I can do, clutching at the pew rail, to restrain myself from uttering some cry of protest or of relief I don't know which, for in the circumstances it is not easy to tell whether this temporary paralysis of the will is a desirable thing yes or no. The scream changes to a gurgle, a sob perhaps, merging with the sound of bells tolling, which instantly dies, struck dumb. Then starts again. The flesh shudders in involuntary spasms the source of which I cannot, for the moment, discover. Is it some mute hunger under whose pressures even the inside of the church now groans in ecstasy: noises such as someone opening doors, shutting cupboards, drawing drawers, dragging loads around. Christ is on the north wall, in an aisle. I look away. The contractor's hand is heavy on the fittings – altar, triptych, rood screen, lectern, pulpit, pews, all seem to have been planned in the account book rather than on the drawing board. As do the railway station, the school hall, the town hall, the post office, the whole church of St John's: a public service built on a tram route, a public utility, like the conveniences. Thick maroon ropes on brass pillars separate a small chapel in the aisle where Jesus slumbers: a tiny altar, a dozen chairs, a strip of carpet, some prayer books. The floor is worn in front of the painting of Jesus, whose caption reads: *If you watch the eyes closely they will suddenly open.*

Would you believe it – it is ten minutes past three and the phone has just rung. I rush down the stairs, it could be you, it couldn't, it could. How my heart is beating – I can feel the pain of the blood shooting along the jugular vein, every muscle in my body has tightened. I can remember what I thought as my hand reached out for the receiver: It's her! The train – how could it be? Perhaps she hasn't gone, something wrong with the train! It was a relief, O God, hearing a man's voice calling my name: Sean! It was only Joss Banks, the fool. O my Darling, the pain of you is too difficult for me. I can't stop the tears any longer. You are gone and I cannot accept this as reality. How I am waiting for you! All day long, from the moment the postman calls, I am waiting for you. I cannot eat; I rush out for a moment to get some boiled shrimps and a bottle of milk in terror all the while that the phone might ring. I am afraid to sleep. How cruel this life is! I do love you so much. I have just got some photographs from Morgan's the chemists. Quite good, but where shall I send them? Your father's address is all I have. Darling, *please don't take my life away.*

Repeating the gesture I had seen him use – cupping and crushing the blue notepaper in both palms – I toss Sean's letter away. It rolls shadowless across the flagstones and comes to rest under the nose of Jesus.

From a locus on the midrib of Sweeley Street, in the centre of an oblique line between the ironmongers and the church of St John's across the way the man with the lilac face idly pivots, now towards the rock, now towards the park. He notes that from this locus in the first direction the crowns of constable, statue, and rock appear to meet on a straight line whose vanishing point is fixed somewhere in the blue, at infinity. He realises that this is not in fact the case: that the crown of the constable is mensurationally lower than that of the statue which in turn is of course lower than that of the rock. In the direction of the park his eyeline penetrates the first-floor windows of the Great Western where from a position in the park, near the fountain, it had rested a while ago below the lintel of the entrance door.

The paper rose. He is unwilling to toss it away though crossing the street he at first drops it into the green litter bin attached to a lamp post outside Marks and Spencers. But immediately, out of a sense of economy perhaps – the flower girls are still rattling money boxes up and down the street – he retrieves the flower. In the bin four equal fragments of a postcard attract his eye. They form a nasty picture – a bulbous blonde cupping her breasts and a half-nude man leave a wood – with a caption that reads: RAIN STOPPED PLAY. The note on the reverse side is meaningless: I have just rushed down the stairs, the telephone rang, but it was the wrong number. Perhaps I haven't told you this before, but ever since I've known you I've had feelings inside me and emotions I never knew existed. You have made a whole man out of me. I know real love, longings, needs, desires, and most of all jealousy! Before, I must have been dead inside, I would never have cried over a woman leaving me... The poem which follows obviously irritates him. As there is now no bin in which to dispose of the fragments – he is already some distance down the pavement heading once more towards the park – he drops them into his pocket.

From the park the ring of geraniums at the foot of the statue cannot, even with concentration and prior knowledge, be seen to terminate the midrib of Sweeley Street beyond the point where the constable in the midst of the traffic should be pivoting on his island. From where now the man with the lilac face observes a teenage couple in oilskin jackets reach the end of Sweeley Street he is beyond the visual threshold, so that asked he couldn't say there is a constable yes or no, an island, a zebra, or whatnot there. But beyond this the eye level visibly rises so that the tipped-up shadows of buildings along that section disclose the oblique interstices of sunlight more precisely than they do lower down the hill where mere inches separate the shadows of buildings one from another. These irregular areas of shadow define by imperceptible stages the incline of the gradient from the park to the rock, from north to south: over the distance their angles of inclination tend to oppose the view rather than to vanish from it. These shadows too by an effect of aerial perspective lighten with recession, so that the purplish blue of the immediate locus pales to musty grey at the foot of the rock along a diminishing scale of tones which at a hypothetical vanishing point beyond the visual field would be lost altogether in atmospheric light. But the visual field is dominated by the grey mass of Trwyn Mawr – grey, gold, ochre, he notes, depending on proximity; even, from certain angles, in certain lights, silver. For the rockface creating innumerable facets of light accordingly at moments glows surfaceless, evanescent, immaterial like a hanging star.

Gwyddr Park is the centre of a star along whose arms traffic moves in every direction. At the centre of this star is a fountain whose crown flowers in iridescent threads of viridian, gold, blue, crimson. Below the centre of this explosion a silver column of water reflects the colours of sky, shadow, the still and moving tatters of the crowd, faces, façades, the clutter of show windows, the girl with the spotted beach ball. She leans over the fountain, she laps her tongue into the water, it arches like a banana. The drops tinkle and splash and escape in a sucking gurgle. She hears multiple rhythms build to a grand rhythm of water, voices, of traffic, which arbitrarily bears this way and that, dissolves into eddies and tangled currents at the whims of the wind, flowing in a directionless stream, swirling back upon itself, bearing left for the promenade, right for the post office and the railway station, circling, wandering, so that wholly carried by this space she is at times its centre, at others its edge or limit. By the centre path of the park the youth is spread-eagled on his spine beside the girl. He agrees, It's nice in here.

His voice attracts the attention of the man with the paper rose. From staring in the direction of Ross's Garage he looks at the pair. Despite the hubbub she confirms: Yes quieter, but immediately she adds, Let's go somewhere. He asks, Where? She gives a wordless shrug. She stares. Façade of Ross's Garage. This red, that yellow; acres of glass, fountain reflected, people.

Inclined at an angle to the direction of her gaze the plate glass of Ross's Garage obliquely reflects the image of Sweeley Street – as it were, ajar. This image impinges upon that of the vehicles displayed on the showroom floor but the register is not spatially exact: that of Sweeley Street refers to a material area larger than the dimensions of the showroom floor extending across the width of the junction and taking in the park, the façades of opposite buildings. These separate groups of images too are mutually exclusive: they do not simultaneously impinge upon the eye. By attending to the contours, the colours and details of the Fords, Triumphs, and Jaguars displayed there the eye relinquishes other images reflected in serial process against the gloom of the showroom walls. The discrimination is automatic, beyond the reach of will. From the centre of the park therefore, or better from a position on the adjacent pavement, the girl might become aware, on the one hand, of a stable picture some thirty feet in depth covering the showroom display or, on the other, of a complex moving panorama extending to almost a hundred yards, defining the activity along Sweeley Street at its junction. But intercepting this image at its centre, in the middle of the park, is that of the fountain whose attributes are these: Through 360° the silver column of water reflects all the life around, moving or still;

the images are threadlike and difficult to discern though the young girl circling the fountain studies them. Resulting from its great velocity the surface tension of the water makes a perfect mirror whose curvature however is so close as greatly to reduce the apparent speed of moving bodies reflected there. A vehicle for example deflecting along Sweeley Street to the right or to the left seems relatively slow approaching that point on the column of water where its reflection is largest, its speed greatest, its position nearest before, simultaneously, it begins to recede and dwindle, its motion becoming slower and slower until the image diminishes in the opposite direction, first to a crawl, then to seeming immobility, and then to extinction.

Not that it is easy to follow the course of a given body through this process, it being often subject to vagaries of its own, sudden stops and starts, unpredictable changes of direction. The visual field too is penetrated by other bodies in haphazard or contradictory locomotion creating interceptions, blockages, pauses, and ambiguities that by extending perception limit the understanding. In addition it is difficult to rein the attention; beckoned hither and thither it is embarrassed by the multiplicity of the data and their conflicting claims, perceptual and emotional. The burden can be overwhelming, so that beyond a certain plane of attention a selective perceptiveness is required, failing which a defensive stupor supervenes depending on the nature of the observer and his interests.

But then the image reflected in the column of water is further reflected – in the young girl's eyes. There beyond her knowledge the image of water is diminished to a thread of light which all but bisects the hazel ambience in which it seems to be buried. The multifarious images of street and traffic with their associated colours and textures are not visible in this reflection though logically they can be conceived still to exist there – the movements of buses say, and other vehicles; of pedestrians, the flight of seagulls, outlines of buildings and so forth that can at any moment be observed in the heart of the fountain, or better *in situ* in their respective positions. The hazel pupil is flecked with a darker brown, the outline of the fountain and part of the façade of the building behind – MORGAN'S THE PHOTOGRAPHIC

CHEMISTS – almost bisected by this vertical silver line which, though, is itself intercepted by the small dark circle of the iris. In this spot the organ reflects nothing at all so long as the girl avoids being dazzled by direct or reflected light from this source or that. Frequently in the course of her observations she needs to blink, or to shade her eyes for just this purpose as the windscreen of an approaching car returns the force of the sun's rays before passing on, or now as a man with a lilac complexion draws from its sheath a curious glittering knife or dagger and examines it, thumbing the edge – a bargain he has doubtless just picked up at the antique shop across the way.

Stabbing into the brow the crown of thorns leaves across the face a web of blood, a dark-veined colouring which could equally well also be a pattern of vessels beneath the skin, an elaboration of chiaroscuro. The style is International Gothic: a Christ that Pisanello could well have envied, down to the blade clenched between the teeth; the blade that could well, I mean, be clenched between the teeth, eyes narrowed to a hair's-breadth. He doesn't look at me. This is possibly, on my part, because of the intensity of tremors, which do not permit a stable vision. Besides which the inside of the church is tearing in the west wind, things straining to come loose. Yet nothing moves. Above the rood screen hangs a dusty gold or orange-coloured flag decorated with a giant appliqué star the colour of blood which has suddenly appeared there, seemingly. The candelabra too whose lights irreverently go on and off are the shape of stars. Did the lights go on I do not know, couldn't say for sure. No, the subaqueous light has never altered though subject to modulation from changes in the brilliance of the day outside. Here there is no agent beside me to interfere with the uninflected gloom. The west wind thumps against the mass of stone but straining for release matter fails to move.

It's true, a voice suddenly exclaims, or gasps, Now isn't that strange!

I do not look at her, but remark: I didn't hear you enter.

I disturbed you, sorry, you were praying?

Coming over dark, isn't it, did you switch on the lights as you came in?

Whatever for, it's quite light enough yet in here.

Beg your pardon, my sight isn't all it could be these days. Now will you switch them on?

There's nothing here you can't see you know, it's not all that dark even outside, in a minute the sun'll be… it's such a brilliant day.

Please do just the same, they're there – behind you – the small room by the font – I think I'm seeing stars or something, you've found them then? That's better isn't it, all on, switch them all on. There, what d'you see?

Hardly makes any difference; it's not been all that dark really.

Thank you. You're very nice. Are you beautiful? Young?

My picture's in the papers, why don't you look up?

What difference would that make, you're hearing me aren't you? How long's it since he – what time is it? – They're still talking about him out there? There's been an accident you know, very serious.

I was there. Is that what's the matter with you then? Some time ago that was, before ten; it's nearly eleven now.

No. There's been another since, haven't you heard?

What other?

Don't people know? Also a man. Why did you come in here, just to escape the crowd?

A seaside place like this you don't try to escape the crowd, you're strange, they're all looking for me anyway, I'm Chloë. After lunch they'll all be out on the prom looking for me: Chloë the Chronicle Girl. Looking for me and me knowing all about it.

Will they spot you d'you think?

Easy to walk in any crowd, very simple, specially when you're being sought. We're much like one another you know, more than you think. You in pain or something? I said we're more alike than you think.

Sorry, yes, I heard that, no, I really can't say; gets cold suddenly in the shade, doesn't it? What're you wearing?

Sleeveless.

Aren't you cold? What if it rains?

I've a plastic mac in my handbag.

Blue.

How did you know?

You're blonde aren't you, skin gold, slender; pretty breasts, wearing a paper rose? I can see your legs. I saw you along Sweeley Street did I not, suppose we make love here, as we happen to be alone – your legs – it's the thought that naturally occurs, isn't it, in circumstances like this?

Whatever for?

To pass the time, is it ever done for any other purpose?

Fancy yourself, don't you?

I know – there's no hurry. We can go into the small room with the switches when we're ready, they hang their cassocks and things in there; those'll come in useful. You've done it before, I should imagine?

I'm married.

Oh, good! Children?

Twice: abortions though, both times.

Suppose you have another?

I've just told you, one man's much like another to me.

Good one, that; you're clever as well as beautiful, I see. So I'm surprised you came here after that painting, there's nothing to it you know. Besides it's very bad – awful thing. By the way, it's ever struck you Jesus never said anything about women? Strange, that, isn't it – not a word; how they're meant to be, I mean?

What would He know about them?

Good girl! Shall we do it now?

We'll play this little game with the painting. Have a look and compare notes, shall we?

Rot! I thought you'd finished with that; haven't you learnt?

I'm not sure you know. I thought I saw them open a while ago, just as I came in, but now I'm not so sure. Must've been the light. Or this postcard. It says on this postcard. It's a strange painting, isn't it!

It's up to you. That's what it's there for. That was a clever poster, by the way, up the road: POLYPLEX. You noticed it? Motorcar tyres, on the left down by the zebra, that's where I first saw you. There's a constable there, isn't there? Is he still there? You went in the paper shop didn't you, wearing a plastic mac. I noticed your legs then, those shoes you're wearing, then after a bit you crossed the road and passed by, close as we are now. Don't belong around here do you? Thought not, no, I'd've noticed you before. Not all that many young people stay around once they can help it – drift you know, nothing to do. You'd bought a picture postcard… and is the constable looking up the hill?

A moment ago you said you couldn't see, now you go on and on.

That's not what I said; it's dark in here that's all, that's what I said and I keep seeing these stars. Feel a bit faint I must admit, but even so it isn't very nice is it?

There's no stars in here.

Use your eyes, Love, there's stars all over the place – the candelabra, that flag up there, can't you see over the rood screen, star of blood on it have a look, plain gold field.

Plain gold is all I see, isn't any star what's the matter with you?

Have it your way we won't argue, you smell like a new-mown cornfield. I live on the edge of a cornfield you know, gold now like a varnished icon, burnt gold, no icons around in here, is there? What a lousy church, eh, should be on the National Health these churches, y'don't think? Really they should get these vicars off their arses to write prescriptions – that'd fill the churches is what I say – daily dose of faith, one needs it.

You're funny, amusing, why don't you look up?

Well that's nice to hear, I'm not often thought amusing but of course you've little to go on, first impressions only actually, haven't you, but then you don't sound all that stupid, you'll learn I expect.

Why d'you say things like that? At school they used to say everybody's stupid in something or other, nobody knows every-thing however educated, that's what I really believe. You shouldn't call people stupid it's wrong; if a person doesn't understand you it doesn't mean he's stupid or anything, you shouldn't talk like that.

There was a small boy once dreamt every night he had to eat the granite mountain outside his bedroom window before day-break, can you imagine that? He'd wake up screaming, spitting real blood in the darkness, terrified of the morning because he might meet this person who set him the task and then he would have to destroy this person, you see.

What's that mean, I don't understand riddles.

I was afraid you mightn't. It's no riddle.

Your belly's making a noise.

Quiet, isn't it, in here? You're ardent, I hope?

What's ardent mean?

You're passionate?

That's always depended on who, who can be passionate with everybody? Can't know until you try, can you?

Shall we have a little trial then on this pew before the real thing as it were? My wife, our first trial was on the kitchen floor but she was someone else's wife then – her husband came in. What d'you think, shall we try? It might take hours, you know, once we really get down to business, we might stumble on this mysterious what's-it they all talk about that's said to last hours or even days.

What did he do to you?

To me? Busted his house up that's all poor chap, one of these people wouldn't put up a fight if you took the shirt off his back.

Made things kinda simple for you then, didn't it?

It never was simple for anybody, such things never are. He killed himself in the end. Now the thing is she can't forget him you see, he's the husband she feels she's always loved. Isn't life just bloody? Situations you see. All blind. What does one do – shall we get down to business then?

Why d'you keep calling it business?

Hard work isn't it, loving?

What if anybody should come?

It's a church isn't it, a sanctum of love?

People mightn't call that love though, might they? Not just any two people never seen each other in the middle of the day.

That's a point, you're very clever; there's at least three kinds of love, I've discovered: Love for Thou, love for Me, love for It – it's not all that much of a piece. The second is all that matters anyway. I'm getting to appreciate you. It won't take a minute, a few seconds even, just for the feel of the thing you know, a trial for aptitude if you like; come on take your pants off.

You need a shave, if y'ask me.

Well now, what's that to do with it?

Well now, what kind of conversation is this then?

Ah, situations…

I don't understand you at all, why d'you suddenly mumble to yourself like that?

What I feel is this, no I won't say that, I'll say this: Once I shot a man – don't worry, there's blood on my hands all right, you'll understand – in a hut, in the war. One of my own men – you must understand that – I didn't want to, it had to be done; we had to get out under fire. He was jabbering with fear, on his knees. He saw himself a dead man, accusing me, offering me his death. I shot him through the head. What I want to know you see is why did it have to be me?

Why bother?

Situations. That's what I'm mumbling to meself about, since you ask; I think about them a great deal – all kinds of ifs, no end. One tries to be fair, to find excuses for the other chap; but it was him or the platoon. Nobody said a word but I couldn't stand their faces. Every day after that I waited for a bullet in the back.

We all go around knowing we could be murdered, so what, you don't keep on about it.

Ah but who wants to die! I wanted to crawl to them to explain. I couldn't stand it, what he was doing to me – that's what I wanted to explain. It was impossible to explain. And I was afraid of them. So I made sure I was extra hard – iron hard – testing them one by one, day by day, a murderee seeking his murderer if you like, till I knew for sure: *They* were afraid of *me*! I could've sung it like a hymn; it was a sort of unsuspected grace people sometimes offer free. But how could you understand? Only then could I bring myself to write condolences to his mother. Understand? Get that situation? *He offered his death –* what more could I say to her? It was a revelation. He wouldn't've died otherwise.

Ought I to be afraid of you then?

You really ought to be of everybody Love, murder attracts us all doesn't it – it's just how we're made and there's nobody free of this power over the next if we only knew. The Poles have a saying for it I understand: Two kinds of men, those with whips and those with wounds. There are no other; clever isn't it!

There's people you can trust and people you can't, and a few of each is more'n anybody's ever likely to know at any time; I don't want to kill nobody, you don't know what you're talking about.

Have it your way.

What makes you talk so superior then – what's it you're so sure about?

Listen. You wake up somewhere you know, middle of nowhere, V-E night. Can't get back to sleep for people yelling, letting off fireworks. Another kind of situation, listen. They're celebrating outside, and there's this hideous woman you've never seen snoring beside you like ack-ack in an air-raid. You don't know her. She's pregnant; she doesn't want the baby. What made you make love to her? There's the sleeping pills you've been thinking about months, years. You've been dead ages – you know that all right. The thing's rotting – you know. You swallow them and lie down waiting. When you make love to her again you feel the baby turn under your belly. She's planning to throw herself down the stairs when they fetch the ambulance. You hardly listen; you won't know anything about it – what'll she feel like in the morning beside a dead lover – I mean your life still smeared all over her skin and thighs and you stone dead beside her. You begin to swear. It's not happening! You're terrified – want to ring people up – who can you ring, there's nobody, there's a war. You rush outside, sweating, walk the streets. People talk. You walk around among them. Christ, you're frightened! They're celebrating. It didn't happen sudden, like you thought – it's not happening – it's not going to happen. You're not dying – you don't know if you're going to die! They're shouting all around you, lighting up the dark. They're happy, yet you can't trust them. Suddenly you see that you can't trust them with your corpse – *that's* the real horror of the thing Chloë, that's what you see. That's what's kept you alive the whole time, just only that – *you can't trust anybody that far.* Try to understand Love. People talk about the fear of death – it's nothing. Dying is nothing at all. I know! It's what your death does to them that people fear… what your corpse does to them… you're young, you don't know the feeling we put into that word – *hatred*!

You won't know anything about it after you're dead so what's it matter?

You know *now* don't you – that's what matters. Therefore you're dying the whole time really, everything else is nonsense. You really didn't understand about the boy and the granite mountain? Can't you see how we're fixed? What's the colour of your eyes by the way, blue?

Look up and see for yourself.

I should've noticed them before, on the road, shouldn't I? You've such a magnificent body you know, most upsetting, what's it feel like?

How?

Trailing excitement wherever you go; most unfair you know, stimulating the public. Oh it's all so lousy! What I think – chaps should walk right up to you and complain: Look Miss, look at what you've done to a perfect stranger. How's a man to have any dignity at all, ever!

I've never heard that's a sin, having a good figure; what's wrong with that now?

No, it's not your fault, it's the way things just are I suppose. Are your eyes blue did you say?

Hazel.

Ah!

Eh?

Excitement again.

What, even without looking?

That's how pitiable we are, you see. There was this scientist could make his dog's mouth water every time he rang a bell.

Well don't start on that again, we're not dogs.

I suppose you can prove that?

Look, can't we just talk sensible?

That a male and a female may never do Love, so it is ordained. In the nature of things you might say.

Off again, aren't you!

Sorry, what shall we talk about then?

We can talk about you?

Just what we've been doing the whole time it seems to me; it all ends up the same way sooner or later anyway. No, having a good figure's no sin, you mustn't think that way; it's mortal power if you like but no sin, power like I've just been talking about if you see what I mean.

Ah-ah! There we go again. Can't you just talk ordinary? You know, you haven't said a thing I understand since from the beginning.

Yet you stay – I'm amazed.

Who *are* you? Just answer me straight.

Self-made, well-off, married, retired – in that order. Straight?

You've said that already. Not in so many words, but you've already told me all that. People your age don't retire, that's what I mean.

True.

Not even when they're well-off they don't retire till they have to.

True again.

You're laughing at me?

I'm not.

Don't laugh at me; a person like you you don't need to. What's your name did you say?

Joss Banks.

Funny name – Joss.

Joshua – sorry. As good as looking up, isn't it, all this cross-questioning.

Well why don't you then? Go on, take a good breath and look me straight in the eyes, I dare you.

No use. I don't want to know you. I'm catching you see. This thing that's dying inside me you might crave it; no, seriously, people do. I just can't carry anybody anymore, Chloë.

You know, you're the most vainest person I've ever met, d'you know that?

You could be wrong of course – I imagine you are – very wrong.

I can hardly hear you, you keep your mouth in your chest.

I have a loud voice naturally; people are often afraid of me. As I've told you I've found it very easy to frighten people for some reason. Always have. Because I've turned stone into bread in my day, perhaps; not so many manage that, do they?

You don't frighten me.

Yet you don't want to make love.

I never said we would.

The point being that we'd be free to go our ways afterwards – it's all the situation calls for you'll agree – I thought you might appreciate that.

You're a gentleman. Just the way you talk. I knew it the moment I came in and saw you praying. Something written all over you but somehow you make me feel strange though. Who are you really? Was it you threw away that scrap of paper on the floor?

Writing paper? Blue?

Sorry, I didn't think you had, I'm sorry I said that. People ought to respect a place like this, oughtn't they?

You're religious.

No, I wouldn't say that.

Superstitious then, one of the two.

Maybe I am, I haven't got a mind like yours if that's what you're driving at. What's your business?

I own a local rag – *The Cambrian Weekly Record* – you won't've heard of it; owned, I mean.

You don't dress the part, I must say; but I suppose you own all sorts of other nice things too, nice house, nice car?

You know, the most powerful thing in the world is not a machine but a woman your age, d'y'realise? No, women rarely do. Priests should all be women like you is what I say, we'd have a real religion then; we'd confess willingly. It's what men need, someone they could really confess to. You've done better in a few minutes than all the people I've ever known put together.

Because maybe you wouldn't let me look at you?

Maybe. But imagine all the world of men blindfold and led around by girls like you, as we should; be most effective, don't you think?

Who would we dress for then? Really, you make me laugh.

Ah! Out of the mouths of babes and sucklings dear girl, you're very sweet. Come hither now, sit by me, you smell like newly mown corn, have I said that before? Blodeuwedd – these Welsh conceive a beautiful woman from the mixture of gaudeous blossoms, that's what you are to me – Blodeuwedd. Thou art not Welsh, methinks?

You're just laughing at me again and I don't like that, you don't really want me, do you?

You needn't expect me to seduce you, if that's what you mean; I can't. That's all over and done with my little goddess, I'm rotting, truly I am, you can only take my word for it I know, but I am, believe me.

Still you… I mean… what's that word you used just now? *Ardent*! You're still ardent, aren't you!

Up to you, that, isn't it; it's not often all that pleasant though, I must say.

Depends.

Oh?

Like I just said, it depends on who. Some meals leave a person hungry, others don't. Fellow made love to me once didn't have no nose at all, but it was the best ever, ever, Oh God!

Interesting.

Just two black holes in the middle of his face and a voice like a ghost.

Why did you then?

I didn't know. Weeks and months he kept following me. He stood under this streetlamp every night just watching me in my room everything I did. First I took no notice of course because of my boyfriend, Gent, liable to come in any minute, then it became so I began to miss him if he was late or didn't turn up. Then one night I couldn't stand it no more; I called him up along the passage by the side of the house and he climbed up on top of the coal shed and I put off the light in my room and slipped through the window. Quite a little drop; he had to grab me round the thighs and it was funny feeling a strange man's arms around your thighs and I'd never even seen his face, funny feeling, sort of frightened and nice at the same time. Straightaway we did it, right there on top of the coal shed. Couldn't talk much, people were eating dinner in the kitchen just there by the window, I could even see them. I kept shooing him not to make a noise but I could still tell from his voice he had something wrong. Horrible. The light from the kitchen window and I could see he hadn't no nose. I couldn't bear to look, but we just couldn't stop; I kept looking away into the darkness but his voice would follow me like a ghost talking. God, how he made love to me! It was just like I'd never done it before the way he made love to me. He must've felt pretty terrible with all that love and only able to crawl out night-time. That's one reason I never allowed him in the room but not only that but because of Gent liable to come in any time like I said. He worked all kinds of shifts, and it wasn't ever really nice with him – too racial – neither of us was getting the most out of it like; he could only get going by calling me white swine and trash and that, so I'd say to him Come on me black baboon you wonderful beast give it to me like you know how, like you give your own women and that would make him so he couldn't help walloping me afterwards – he just never could keep his hands off me then – because who was I laughing at and I used to tell him lots of people got kinky hair down there he'd been in this country long enough to know, wasn't any point him taking up that attitude, not because he was the only man I'd ever loved he should think he could do it better than anybody else, and he asked who's this anybodyelse, and I said other chaps I used to know before because I couldn't tell him about the man on top the shed could I? And then after that he began making love to me in his railway uniform because one night he come home and I said it made him look manly, he come to bed with this duffle-coat and oilskin cap and make love to me shouting British Rag British Rag British Rag to the end, and he had a voice on him that man, and me shrieking Baboon Baboon Baboon and going crackers really just to keep him steamed up if y'know what I mean. That's why I run away – we was driving each other up the wall and there wasn't no fun in it really except we keep insulting each other. Even though I wanted his children, I really did, I always will I think, I never wanted anybody's children after that, only abortions.

Yet you got married.

People like you do so why not, everybody ends up doing it. All these wrinkles on your neck, it's stupid hiding your face like that, I could just stoop down if I like and look, couldn't I? I could just sit here till you get tired of it; what's the use anybody trying to hide his face, what's the use in that, it's so stupid; even if you didn't have no nose or anything you shouldn't mind about people all that much they're not even looking half the time, who the hell're they anyway to make a fuss about?

That's no problem – people – you can't live without people. I am there because there's the other, ever heard that one? – wisdom from a dead friend you might call that. No, why I don't want to know you is I don't want to spoil us being together; we don't know how to meet without killing each other you see. I was dying for somebody and you came, it's so beautiful… it can't remain that way once we meet, it's how things are. Us Europeans we conceive goddesses. You'd simply begin to die the moment I seduce you; you're young yet, you can't know; no, someone else must be your murderer – why've we made it this way I wonder?

You don't wish to make love to me then? I wasn't even thinking about anything like that before I came in here, now you've made me so I can't help meself.

That's another matter. Nor was I before you came in. It's a terrible story that – about that dog – don't you think?

Nobody's a dog.

Have it your way.

Oh, I could just listen to you talk all day long you're so… the things you say… Your voice is like cello music d'y'know that Joss? You're beautiful… just so beautiful…

More fool you fair maid.

The man with the lilac face leaves the small group of persons standing outside Ross's Garage staring at the wrecks deposited in the yard. These have been placed so that the sight of them would not inhibit the trade in new cars in the showroom display. But for the haphazard crossings and recrossings of pedestrians, the pauses and spontaneous changes of direction, the blockages and interceptions created by the movement of vehicles along Sweeley Street he could keep in his gaze in the mirror of the fountain any object or person occupying the visual field within a radius of 180° behind without changing his position over the bronze bowl and simply at most by minute adjustments of the angle of incidence of his gaze on the surface of the cylinder. But this is so only, he perceives, in theory. For even granted its explicit diminution with

distance a host of unpredictable contingencies continually interfere with the identity of a given image: the action of sun and
shadow, the silhouetting of light upon dark, the merging of dark
with dark, transient fusions, temporary obfuscations resulting
from the varying intensities of light. Colours in motion behave in
a manner which is independent of the masses to which they refer,
he observes: they do not for one thing recede with the perspective
precision of material bodies. Thus it is that, observing the minute
pageant inside the column of water, he allows his attention to slip
from this object to that in accordance with its visual significance,
its movement, its prominence. It is a game. In so far as he
consciously enjoys it it is a game and nothing more.

No sound moreover is associated with these movements to
lend a greater importance to one image over another: there is only
chance contiguity, haphazard continuities, incongruous relationships, wayward associations. And these associations are often
as subjective as they are actual. So that from moment to moment
he hardly remembers those happenings or conjunctions which
had held his attention, even his interest, a while ago, it being a
dumb show, precisely speaking, without core or meaning.

This much must be added; persons pursuing their business
along Sweeley Street, their business or their pleasure, pay no
attention to the projection of their actions, their activities, their
movements, upon the visual field. Naturally. It is as though from
the sanctum of the insulated "I" all the world were thought to be
blind; as though this "I" were not itself constantly multiplied on
a thousand moving retinas, each from a different angle, and
thereby modified. Yet all is motion, reflection, modification,
multiplication: Sweeley Street as it were observing Sweeley
Street. Barring context there is no meaning, no pattern; except for
the untidy flight of seagulls there is only earthbound horizontality,
wilful and repetitive motion between point and point. The
surface of Sweeley Street with greater or lesser liveliness in parts,
in a manner of speaking, crawls. But even this restricted flow,
taken for granted, can be arrested in the batting of an eye into a
frozen picture of multifarious and absurd postures. Time, withdrawn from activity, discloses motion suspended – intention,
promise – as in a snapshot, as on a Grecian urn: legs arrested in

scissor action, a mouth agape, a gesturing arm, a turning neck, a torso bent. Most strikingly distance becomes material, space congeals so to speak, between arrested bodies – gaps do not open or close, the double-decker no longer bears down upon the cycling club, it holds its distance: its distance holds it back. This materialisation of space occurs, however, only within a fixed radius of a given locus, beyond which gaps diminish with distance, persons become people, people a crowd, a crowd a mass, diffuse at its edges, seemingly immaterial, in the nature of a cloud or phantasm for all the mind can grasp: a term, a limit, a threshold to some further state. It is surprising too how rapidly a body surrenders its identity, merging into the general ambience – three or fourscore yards, no more, beyond which it becomes impossible to recognise even intimate relations, wives or lovers. Surprising, alarming even, when the mind thus perceives the visual constriction within which human personality manages to operate, and even to flourish. Granted which isolation of the eye a relative insulation ought perhaps to be allowed for, with corollary convictions about the blindness of the world, limitations of space, futility of time, et cetera.

The double-decker bears down upon the cycling club. The images in the fountain vanish as the person with the lilac face again crosses the street and walks towards the rock. The bus closes upon the last of the cyclists – yellow stripes and black – and commences to overtake the line, who to a man are free of the saddles straining uphill though as far as the roundabout where the constable now just comes into view the gradient is not steep. Inches from his eyes a blur, a neck, a shoulder, stops, turns: You should've taken the small ones, I told you. Over this shoulder across the way a man's head bobs a few times up and down. His lips cannot be seen. His wife or friend stares at him but nothing can be seen either of her face. Comparatively speaking they seem minute, hardly more than the height of a head, but this is only relative; the couple assume more normal proportions the moment they can be viewed in isolation: in instances when with an effort they can be observed free of the interference of persons passing close at hand. But movement along the pavement is dense.

The distance begins to open between the tail of the bus and the head of the line of cyclists, now grey. The latter seems with the opening gap to be moving slower and more slow, almost to be moving backwards.

Better to observe the actions of the couple across the way it would be necessary for one standing by the show window of the ironmongers opposite the church of St John's near to the library to move forward, free of passers-by, five or six paces to the kerbstones. Four paces, he finds, going one way, but four and a half strangely, going the other. This is either on account of the difficulty of treading the same conceptual straight line twice, or due to variations in the length of single paces, the latter depending on the activity of the mind, or on the closeness of the attention, from moment to moment. Then a hollow quivering scream is heard which instantly dies, apparently from the interior of St John's; due to the traffic roar it is not easy to say. The couple on the opposite pavement move on. No one is concerned over the blonde woman who rushes onto the lawn from a door in the north aisle arranging her dishevelled bosom, with backward glances. Her expression of shock is disguised as she grapples with the church gate. On the pavement she slackens her agitated pace to a walk that matches the rhythm of the crowd but in front of Marks and Spencers she stops, takes from her handbag what appears to be a blue paper ball, and drops it into the waste bin attached to a lamp post there. Then her figure is swallowed up in the dense movement of pedestrians approaching the zebra, in the direction of the rock.

Right here it was, the pregnant woman informs her husband. That's where the blue Ford was, and that's where he came off the kerb you see, all in the twinkling of an eye.

True, the pair of strident skidmarks record on the tarmac what was perhaps the last conscious action of the youth in the Mini-van; skidmarks and a naked gash or two which reveal the woodblock foundation of Sweeley Street. Every other trace of tragedy has been removed: the blood and oil, the fragments of glass, and of course the wreckage.

And that's the church. What I think about that painting, see, it's no trick like they say; like I said, He can open His eyes only by *you* wanting Him; He's as good as blind otherwise. And even when He does it's for you alone not for anybody else; every man must try for himself, you see, if he wants the love of Jesus.

But the man can see no need for this Christly gimmick. He says so. He adds: You get some of these folks they're *born* blind, what about them then?

He considers the whole damned thing tourist ballyhoo and nothing more.

10.30–11.07

Tom's statement claims that knowing the works blindfold Titch was unlikely to have had an accident there in broad daylight. It was true of course that there had been a similar accident in the press room a fortnight ago, but what more did that signify than someone's carelessness! Titch had no reason voluntarily to plunge his head into the boiling crucible, business for one thing had been topping anything known in Joss Banks' time. It could hardly be thought on the other hand that Titch's deafness had contributed in any way to the tragedy, Titch was easily the most alert person Tom had ever known. He hoped Titch had not lost his mind permanently, or worse, for Titch only could give the exact truth. In the meantime had Joss Banks been invited to make a statement?

It is an indifferent painting by a minor *Fauve* but the carnival theme interests me, the vivid contrasts, bitter discords. European painting simply cannot survive this displacing of chiaroscuro by pure chromatics, chiaroscuro being the very essence of our northern vision – thus spake Lho – soon we shall come to tinted vapours and suchlike, then what! But as to Sandra's postcard all is light, that much can be said for her taste – unequivocal, frontal, impersonal light. The procession crawls across the beach clenched in this light towards the rock, towards the hungry surf. In the foreground umbrellas, beach balls, a purple nude, all taut, faceted, glowing like crystal cut. Crystal horizon, crystal everywhere, gems sparkling in wave crests, on each glassy pebble, on each particle of silica in the sand, on cottage windows that spangle the face of Trwyn Mawr. Cerulean sky, ultramarine sea, polished incandescence beyond the Caedmon hills. The shadows of the promenade, of the promenade shelters, lamp posts, tide clock, life-ring stanchions, of the hotels along the front, of the craggy mass of Trwyn Bach, change to vaporous blue drenched in light, blurred at their cores, sharp at their edges, sombre with the blue richness of land, space, sea. The fortress of mossy rocks begins to dry out, and the little pools and wonders left back by last night's tides return irregular shimmering patches to the sky. It is as much as one can do, for the hollow drumming wind, to attend to the tinkling sound of wavelets, metallic almost and ringing, inorganic, unevenly washing the foot of the beach, clinging to the rocks, retreating. From the rocks, from the sharp edges of the promenade, from the jetty, the pier and every upstanding thing there is an accelerated silver whistling as of air sucked dry and screaming across desert sands – fitful, untidy, immense, every direction scored with the haphazard geometry of seagulls and their abrasive shrieks. VISITORS ARE REQUESTED IN THEIR OWN INTERESTS TO REFRAIN FROM FEEDING THE BIRDS. Affronted, the birds menace each other, simultaneously respond to explosions from the quarry inshore, describe interlocked cages of space suspended at migrant points between Trwyn Mawr and Trwyn Bach, so that the immense aerial network of their flight defines the dimensions of the bay, delimits a space within the greater space of horizon, sea, hills; or, reversing the image, the inshore detonations lie at the heart of a hemisphere within which the limits of the bay are fixed at determined but migrant points so that there is a universal and a local sound, a local and a universal space. The local space moreover is differentiated in depth and extension by the variegated mingling of people now appearing on the beach, planting umbrellas, windbreakers, folding-chairs, creating purple shadows, fresh contours, new surfaces, the entire panorama fragmented. The local sound is qualified by voices, by the cries of small children, the occasional barking of a dog, the movement of traffic along the promenade, the bells of the Gwyddr Fair, the universal whistling of air across and through the rocks, the drumming of wind and sea, the relayed cycles of sound issuing from the quarry shredded and torn about the ears and reshaped into an intimate mosaic whose quality ceaselessly changes from moment to moment. A combine harvester, for instance, hums on the limits of the aural threshold, a train at the junction – a diesel, no; on the crown of Trwyn Bach an aluminium pylon glitters, could be, left there by the RAF or somebody years; there is no humming, no threshold, no thing that is not; he thinks the blonde in the bikini as brown as a black and that's not all, a black with blonde hair who's to say reflected wiggly-woggly in the wet sand, space between the thighs like a seagull. To the shadow of the rock along the beach there is as much bare flesh surface for surface as there is sand, earthbound, horizontal mostly, from a distance horizontal but contorted really, foreshortened, compacted cheek by jowl, breathing deep regular breaths, that's what the humming is, life's-breath unforced, lungs and aesophagi throbbing with it all over the place, prodigal,

113

concerted. The concert of life, nobody's ever thought of that, ai, singers measure for measure adding their jots and tittles to the grand huzza, no little squeak too faltering, too humble or inept though unacknowledged; it is the song is it not not the singer not the song it's the spirit that counts, the willing gesture of the tone-deaf, of the dumb, of dogs, hippopotami, all the upper and lower kingdoms, cuttlefish, starfish, nauplii, each its little dumb howl. The woman is called Pamela in an educated voice: *Pam*la! Her man sits on the pebbles under a wooden pier, black trunks, smoking a pipe. Pamela turns beneath her hair, which from streaming behind now cups her face. Her long plain face. Here we have to do with the robust youth of love, its blood-red ardours, for by a silent nod behind the pipe she is made to know that her child is crying, sure enough, on the prom in a pram, adding his feeble might, mite, to the universal howl. With a tired shrug Pamela shuffle-slaps the pebbles to the source of her joy, her comfort, her pride. And should the good youngster be befouling the virgin air, it is not more, one way or another, than he is set to do (and very well equipped) for ages yet to come, he and his penis and unsuspecting progeny. And should his puny protests be unavailing, who does not know that they never will avail, never do more than fret and tear. Dead lucky he would be. Pamela knows that he was born but to murder her, the fruit of her womb, bestowing brief fusions of understanding along the way, brief interludes in which, beholding the menace in her horse's teeth he would consent to suckle at the breast screwing and jabbing at it in a frenzy of disbelief; called love. But make it once clear that she never was meant to eat him the brute cavorts in ever new guises, standing on his own four feet as it were, unfettered, thanking no one for who is there to thank. His father has vanished. Everyone gravitates to the rock, sooner or later, drawn thither by sympathetic attractions perhaps, perhaps the hubbub, life compressed calling as it does to life, overspilling into the North Atlantic eyes ever landward, the life boat from the West Shore ever ready. But what of the swimmers on the West Shore? They follow the life boat, hence the crowd. That's not true. People do swim on the West Shore, from whence they are more frequently called to the horizon, the ignorant, the brave. Not that the sirens are silent ever at the foot of the rock, we mustn't give the wrong impression, conditions are much the same in either place, it being the same sea, same beckoning deeps, same rock, same flowering island; let us not colour the facts, they have their own cold dignity, indestructibility. In season the numbers beckoned are about equal, it isn't easy to say offhand, one should ask. And that's Caedmon only. What about the rest of the Welsh coast, the girdling island coast? Well, what of it! Unprovoked alarums wherever you look, listen rather, you needn't stop; alarums compacted, aeons ribbing the face of Trwyn Mawr, bare rock bone dead, fusions of space, valleys ineffable, he who runs may read, tripping over his furious entrails the while, brave.

To the face-worn image distorted now at the sagging end and chapter's close in the universe of the copper pipe he might be uttering an ancestral No! What else in all conscience is to be made of the taut lips, the floriate brow, grey eyes whose wrinkles seem barely to counter the effects of gravity, for surely now, surely those tired eyes yearn only to the solace of the bags under them settled there, he swears, just these past three years or so, three years refusing to settle forever, to be what has been, has been lived, is formed and finished; the eyes of a sorcerer instinct with the spectacle of his apprentice trapped in mature and senseless skills, or of the architect who lives to address alas his youthful edifice converted to incongruous stone – cathedral say to power-station – while still exploiting his virgin gesture and name. He sees his father's corpse. He feels in his bloodless sorrow, shame. At this incomprehensible defeat of virility. The tears of his mother he cannot accept, they do not count, he does not therefore comfort her. For this is not her grief, he sees, but his, a grief of men; not a loss but a rejection which lies in the moment of his grasping, reflectively, the stem of his father's bud for that assurance which certain peoples know in gorging on the grey matter of a dead king, the transference of ancestral substance, ancestral bud, ancestral substance incorporate in the cult's original bond and charter; leaves, pebbles, animal bones, bleak mud from the river – an assurance that power is infinite and impersonal, that flesh goes naked back to earth, that within the human assonance rejection is impossible, that death and birth, departure and arrival, exit and entrance are but seemingly opposed, that banishment is the ultimate and only curse since what man may survive a wilful and arbitrary abstention from this original bread, man being bred in every sense that matters, of man? But in his hand rejected he grasps only mute flesh. He drags the foreskin back and worries the last drops into the urinal, thereafter for some moments continuing to grip his orphan organ uncomprehending; for compressed to the thickness of the copper pipe and echoing its curvature the rejected image exhorts: But you are beautiful! His smile shrinks into burnished metal, hallowed grave of thought (and how far might one credit this distortion of the image, this mean illusion, even allowing for the vagaries of the reality which permits it: the subaqueous glow from the pavement-lights, the erect posture compacted in the curvature of the lavatory pipe which from wall to wall against the virgin tiles registers his name and habit, rebellious grave-clothes, to the shoe tips – Joss Banks! – his name proud as mail and as infertile, fecund nonetheless with faith for life will behave will it not as though it cannot end; faith, fear, what else? – no, not hope – and fear of what or whom, and why)? There is the quiet rasp of his zip-fastener (yet in the corrugated space he does not move) the rasp, the whimpering disinfected air warm in his nostrils; he clings to his limp skin and evidence, his sacrament and sign, his votive stone.

A man may perceive the error of God and yet not budge!

Thus the festal image burgeons in a mien of scorn torn free.

Beyond the bar the mirror duplicates the visual field where laughter thick with cloud exploits a condition of sound, there and not there, of which one's very self may well be author and centre, a function of space and yet not space, as the membrane is a function of the drum yet not the drum, around and through yet distinct, as the interior bone of skull bears in itself the web and sign of the grey matter it imprisons, the shape of thought or being whose impress, evident only in dissolution, is beyond cognition or verification, the fruit and dereliction of time, a bitten laughter, carved and bitten bone of laughter for which, who knows – and how could he slumped on the bar-stool not know – there is no evidence, no sign, no author or authority, no reference, a meaningless geometry. The mirror beyond the bar duplicates this constricted visual field. Painted on its surface like sign or fence or barrier for the unwary is an advertisement, SKOL: the limit of the tangible, the verifiable, the point beyond which begins mere light, illusion. But it is an ordering of light so exact in tonal fidelity (and yet so immaterial) that painters sometimes use mirrors to correct the object by its reflection – each smallest detail, distorted by familiarity or by ignorance, measured against the disembodied image, the illusion. Thus the image corrects its referent, illusion modifies reality; the creature, paradoxically, judges its creator. The verdict is verifiable always, for are they not bound creature and creator and in spite of themselves, in that most despairing state of all love – faith?

The eyes of the pregnant woman fall on those in the mirror. He *is* watching her she's certain now, studying her, as he has done all the morning. The tired grey eyes with bags under them. He is unshaven, thickening around the jowls. He is respectable, he looks a tramp. Abruptly she says to her husband: Let's go from here, there's evil in this place somehow, I want to go.

Come on Love, just a minute, just a minute.

I don't like it here anymore, come on, let's go, I mean it.

Chap down the road this morning popped his head in boiling oil, did you hear? Now, I ask you!

Ai, what's the world bloomin' coming to! It's all this affluent strife, if y'ask me, this well-fed state, they never had it so tight.

Makes you think, dunnit?

Joss! Didn't you hear me calling you then?

Sorry, Sean, such a bloody row.

What bloody row? Isn't hardly nobody around, it's early yet. Where's that letter, I dropped it in the bin outside Marks', you took it didn't you?

Letter?

Come on then, you know what I'm talking about, blue notepaper. Where in hell does rubbish get to?

It *was* rubbish then, wasn't it! Forget the woman.

I want it Joss, there's terrible things in it; I don't know what I said, I must be out of my mind.

You threatened to do yourself in, why don't you, she'll never come back; she's lost every one of your frenchies too by now, two or three each night, that's for sure. Now leave me alone, you slob.

Swine! What in hell's matter with you today, you look bloody awful.

I dropped it in the church. Sanctum of love, what time is it?

Dunno.

Heard about Titch?

Poor sod, yes; bloody awful.

Mightn't live, might he – pretty serious I mean, not much they can do about extensive burns, you know. Have a brandy.

No, I must go get it straightaway Joss, thanks a lot.

Tell you something.

When I get back; I won't be a mo'.

Hey!

What?

I just met the Chronicle bitch; lovely bit of skin.

But she isn't around till four, surely?

In a bed-and-breakfast around here somewhere I expect, wish I knew, I saw her down the road, no, in the church, met her in the church.

Funny meeting anybody in a church?

We just met. I went there feeling sort of sick – what's it y'trying to say? – feeling like bloody death; could've been your boiled shrimps I think. In she comes looking for this picture – that thing of Jesus. We get to talking, talk a lot, but I keep feeling sick, seeing stars, couldn't hardly carry the weight of me head. The old barrel kept making a noise too, she said.

So it is right now; too much tipple.

It's me ulcers I say, and she falls for that. I wish it *was* ulcers, sometimes, sometimes months on end, I don't know. Something been coming and going in my mind a lot you know, on and off, happened last summer up Trwyn Mawr I don't understand. It's like this: You're driving along up there minding the slopes and bends, yes? – there's nothing but those the whole way is there: sea, seagulls, rock, sky. Suddenly there's somebody all crumpled up on the road ahead. You try to swerve, but just that much of course and you're over the top, so you don't swerve enough.

You're braking with all your might – forty, fifty, nothing much you know – but there's no time. You come to a stop on top of his face. The skol pops like a balloon, *plop*! It's a small boy. He might've been dead or alive before that, you don't know, you'll never know. You break out in a sweat, understand? Sweating on the palms. You've got to get out before the next chap comes along. Practically paralysed with fright but you can't tear yourself away; it's leaving that body behind, see. You run back up the hill; halfway you suddenly want to hide, you've got to hide. You can't. Christ! You know you've just got to get back *there* – something's pulling you back. Up the rock, hands and knees, tearing your clothes and skin, I lost a shoe, up to the spot where he would've fallen bird's-nesting – that's what happened. Every summer the same, these kids. Down below there's all the cars going round the curve. The body's there, he's dead but even so it doesn't happen again. You see? It doesn't happen to anybody else. Now how's that Sean, they all come pelting round the curve, but they see it in time. *It doesn't happen to them!*

It does though you know, you're wrong, things like that keep happening to people the whole time. You should've stopped there and waited for help of course.

See? It's not what I'm talking about at all. Right. Maybe. Maybe not. But it's not what I'm talking about. Nothing would've changed by me hanging around, would it? He was dead. I took away bits of his face on the car; I found them sticking there later, looking for my shoe. That's not what I'm talking about. Up in the Kirikiri Hills, in the war, I nearly stepped on a mass of pulp with a head on it begging me to put it out of its miseries. It isn't what I should've done then or not done; all I want to know is *why me!* He was just a smear in the sand, pulp, as I say. I shot him. The flies settled back in a purply greeny veil. Then I left it there with this gaping great hole in the skull. And why did I shoot him d'you think, to put him out of his miseries? Not on your nelly. What could that mean to me, I mean honestly? There was bodies all over the place rotting. He would have died the same if not for me, so might I. I shot him *because he made it happen to me*, understand that Sean? One of these situations, if y'get my meaning – all pat and ready – all I had to do was *arrive*. There's a man somewhere waiting to do it, to do such a thing to a victim he's never seen – a non-man. Out of the blue this non-man was *me*! He offered me his death like a whore her cunt; I mean what's in it! What's a chap to do! Christ I could scream sometimes, don't go yet Sean, don't go, have a drink. No, you get the feeling well who the hell's doing it – why can't a man be left alone! I can't find excuses for other people. What's their excuses?

You're being bloody morbid all of a sudden aren't you, what the hell's come over you?

Keep looking back, if only this, if only that, it's killing. Listen to this one. No, I won't say that, but it brings you up short sometimes, can't see the way forward what to choose; no reason to go one way more'n another, no reason. Titch this morning, I don't understand. Who's responsible for the bloody formula Sean? I mean you'd want to tear the bugger's balls out, wouldn't you?

You're just being middle-aged Joss, you want to cut this thing about being scared growing old, it's killing you, take a hold on yourself. This Chloë, what's she like then, dark? fair? Hundred quid isn't it, or five hundred?

Lovely, ai! Don't feel all that good you know suddenly; couldn't be your boiled shrimps no serious the muck they sell these days, don't they! Hundred quid Chloë she told me, no she didn't, I read it somewhere; must be a hundred, Chloë, yes hundred quid. Worth two any day. Have a brandy. The shit they offer these days, really. Let's drink to your bitch's lido-green... Sean, I think I'm going to puke or something, wouldn't that be awful. There's a chap was killed along here this morning, young fellow, full of beans, let's drink to him, ai, let's drink to the dead, show you who's scared; I *know* death me boy.

He's dead then?

So they keep saying, have a double on him, yes?

You're bloody depressing today Joss, isn't it bad enough?

Never mind Adonis, we drink to your bitch's lido-green... she'll never know, there's things I want to say to you, you've no idea what the word means, depressed; you've lost your bit of fanny, that's all, that's not depression; you get these bouts of self-pity that's all right but it ain't depression me lad, not by a long

120

chalk it ain't. The bitch's skedaddled, she might come back she might not, things won't be the same again anyhow. Another bitch'll come along, chap like you you could have one of them in Boots' or Woolworths tonight if you want it; after a while you will too, there's nothing stopping you is there, young and free, nothing's stopping you. You'd kill yourself if she doesn't, so you say, but you won't, all you need is a good hard now and then then you're ready for the next bitch that offers.

You can't be told anything can you you win every time, nobody can tell you anything. *You* can't tell me if I love my woman or no, *I love her!*

Awright I know I know don't shout; you'll learn that only a good hard now and then can bridge this gulf between a man and a woman, you'll learn.

She's a liar, thief, tramp, skedaddles with my frenchies, I love her. That's what's her.

You love her making you suffer, you nut, that's remorse that. Any bitch comes along makes you feel a bit of remorse you beat her up and call it love. And I can tell you why you don't want any bitch you can't beat up. You won't have a bitch like that because *you're* scared, same's everybody else, scared stiff of the cunt'll come along one day with teeth! Ai, they gobble you up, suck you in, castrate a man the bitches. You either wallop them and call it love or come a cropper squirming between their legs, don't you! Christ, what a long deal this life's-breath.

Comes then an image some time forming, clear now, clear in his mind of the fog of smoke, suddenly focused, of the pregnant woman staring in fascination, repugnance, he couldn't say, at him, beside her husband's profile. Rising – it is the movement that takes his notice – she clears the table, grazing chair-backs, sidling, squeezing, approaching the bar. In one hand three glasses, an ashtray with a fragmentary picture postcard in the other, now looking elsewhere than into the tired grey eyes, for the thousandth time perhaps at the mirror, at the coloured advertisement painted there, SKOL. Men at the bar heedlessly backface in every direction; shoulder over shoulder, arms, necks craning. She tiptoes, bumps, curves contact, crush, squash, a hip, a shoulder, elbow, the knees suddenly of the man with the tired eyes who in the privacy of the crowd asks harsh so that she starts: So what *you* staring at, what's it then? Lips firm, stubble-grey cheeks loosening, grey eyes keen with bags under them. There this woman enters the man, dwells there briefly as in a familiar element, whispers astonished: Somewhere I've seen you somehow, on the telly somehow or something? Your face, ah yes, I've got it. Gosh, the painting in the church… the spitting image…

He grabs Sean by an arm, quaking. Do me a favour, will you old man? Hang on a bit, don't leave me. But immediately then he adds, hopeless: Never mind, not a damn anybody can do about anybody. Fear's only fair after all, how's that? See you later, friend.

Under his eyes the bags visibly fold into deeper shadows. On the glossy black surface of the bar the publican has arranged the four equal fragments of the picture postcard brought in by this pregnant woman: a bulbous blonde with a half nude man leaves a wood clutching at her breasts above a caption that reads: RAIN STOPPED PLAY. It does not amuse him but urgent words scribbled across the legs of the lovers lead him to turn the card over. At the note written there his face lightens in an interested smile: I have just rushed downstairs – the telephone rang, but it was the wrong number. Perhaps I haven't told you this before, but ever since I've known you I've had feelings and emotions I never knew existed. You've made a whole man out of me. I know real love, longings, needs, desires, and most of all jealousy! Before, I must have been dead inside, I would never have wept over a woman leaving me. Is my life to go on endlessly/Wanting you so much/I'll keep my love for you/Until the end of time/ For I am truly happy/Knowing you are mine/The beauty of your body/And the passion that it holds/Delights me beyond reality/I am happy Dearest Lover/ That you belong to me. Darling *please don't take my life away.*

An expression of thoughtfulness you might say, perhaps of understanding or even of respect, rapidly replaces that of amused interest on the publican's face. Finally he smoothes the fragments and drops them into his pocket. For some moments thereafter he continues to stare into space.

The lilac complexion deepens to purple around his nose and malar bones, so that close at hand the surface of his fair skin seems vaguely kaleidoscopic: pink, lilac, purple with a suggestion of blue or green where a pattern of veins frills the hollows of his cheeks. Thin lips, pale blue eyes, mouse-coloured hair which, standing before the full-length mirror in the lavatory beneath Gwyddr Park, he combs in uniform strokes straight back from his forehead. The comb is dry but even so the strands of hair easily obey its distribution and set off his lean nervous face. In the mirror is reflected the panel of doors behind him, each its polished brass lock and a penny slot on one of which can be read ENGAGED. His figure is illuminated by a glacial glow from the pavement lights above and this modifies the colours of his dog-tooth check jacket, cream shirt, gold-coloured necktie, the paper rose in his buttonhole which out of a sense of economy perhaps (the flower girls are still rattling money boxes along the length of Sweeley Street) he still wears. Framed in the mirror his image is as chromatically rich as those of the figures of saints in the windows of St John's or the pasteboard images in the amusement arcade across the way from which he has just been observed to depart. It is the conversation of a group of schoolboys using the urinals beside him which seems abruptly to direct his attention to the various acts of sexual union figured on the green paintwork before his eyes for the words Act of Union several times occur in their discourse, along with the date 1536 and various other historical facts which might be thought to baffle his understanding, for the boys in fact pay no attention to the obscene mural crowned with a hysterical confession that immediately focuses his attention: I BELIEVE IN GOD! raggedly scored to the naked concrete, a juxtaposition of the sacred and the profane that he has hardly time to ponder in the halflight before inches below his eyes light on another, a surly threadlike scrawl, a lonely and cynical manifesto: I BELIEVE IN CUNT! solemnly defiant.

This literature evokes a reflective expression on the lilac countenance, an expression it might almost be said of meditation.

He knew at last that he would ring Bid; it wasn't helping any not facing that fact. Which is this: If you mean never to go back to your wife there are little things to be discussed usually, usual when you've left after violence, words, years of words, nearly three, for when was it Lho had hanged himself? Two Septembers before the last, now July. In certain cases of course there is no need: when there is the other woman for instance. You avoid it then, naturally, as is only to be expected.

But Sean finds him: he is being sought. Ah now the flower of creation they'll run him squirming up the rock, split and bruise his sides, for his spirit what can they do to that, what spirit anyway, to beds of bloody roses crowned with thorns and fangs with frantic questionings. They. Who never bothered bargaining for kingdoms, who never were offered but a crust and plank, two planks making one gibbet or cross or stay that is, to comfort their humming hearts. All Sean says though is that there was no letter there in the darkness, on the naked flagstones, no word, nothing to hold the eye but shadows, the splintered face of Jesus. What then? Scour the pavements, the gutters, the litter bins along the street, love might who knows be found discarded there among the detritus, indestructible like matter, one can be proven wrong. Where there's a will there's a wallop yet.

And then he flees. He flees at a frozen lick more urgent than even panic ensures. There is a circled sky flecked with summer (shimmering rays of hope), a seagull marks his shoulder, a weightless white burden. Bland hotels, carnival streets, beach balls in spots and stripes and whatnot, patterns of crowd pressing, criss-crossing, penetrating one another in a motion that takes them simultaneously forwards, backwards, sideways like ducks on a pond, innocently humming. They. He is encapsulated in a motion, in a surge engulfed. He, it is the sober truth, takes to his heels. Being only human. Has he forgotten alas that one can tread unobserved in any tumult, men being, as he was told not so long ago, so very much alike? He has not forgotten this no, to give him his due. He still has some wits about him, the last blunt edge of human cunning it has not worn quite away, not in his twoscore years or so. He runs, fear being, to be sure, merely fair. The Big Wheel rotates stark against the sky like a forsaken gibbet. Might the Big Wheel thus endlessly turn as does the earth? 50°... 60°...longitude east, et cetera, 80°...90°...100°...to the end of time? He doubts. Stops running. They. Their eyes never come to rest; they light indifferently on this object or that, this person or that, without curiosity, without satisfaction, not knowing when they've had enough. Why then does he run. Whither run. It is an island, is it not, bone and bane, bounded by beckoning deeps in spite of instant communication, the arteries of the railways? Instant communication! He comes up short outside a phone booth in the midst of himself breathless: Bid! Listen Bid, I'm in a town are you

What did you say?

They.

Joss, haven't you got them then?

That's what I mean, I'm just going to. Have a heart Bid, he won't let me have them, copyright you know. Bid! Don't be angry Love, he's hard – have you heard I've had to knock him over the head I don't mean that I didn't mean that he's had an accident I mean

Joss!

He made it happen, Love.

You'd better come right up here at once.

He doesn't, however. Sweeley Street glitters. The rock hangs like a star in the noonday sun. Sharp edges meet sharp shadows with a quality of sound, a continuous grinding jubilation and flourish as of harps and cymbals in the air, of song, of unheard bells, of just audible airs and antique graces; the song of birds, at intervals, in the traffic. At intervals: as a general thing the birds venture no closer to the coast than the woods at the foot of the gleaming hills of Caedmon, inland. Unceasing though the cry of seagulls, brazen, imperious. In gaps and pauses these creatures like everyone else take a turn along the midrib of Sweeley Street simply, it might be thought, for the taste of the thing: they have no obvious calling there.

Is he dead, then?

It is thought that the man in the Mini-van was not a long time dying. The baker, the butcher, the whoever he asks they cannot say for sure, they think he might be dead by now. What is life, they ask in turn. A bauble, that's life, the more irreverent say.

Tom. He rests the telephone when Joss enters. Joss enters; enters, as of yore, Joss's name: Banks Press, Job Printer, Photo Engraver, Commercial Designer, *The Cambrian Weekly Record.*

Tom is boss-eyed. His sight is good nevertheless, insights scrupulous. He smirks: That you Joss?

What does he mean?

Hell'va season this, they're all over the place. Thought you might've gone to lunch.

How y'mean – circulating today, aren't we?

Ah Tom, Tom, good old Tom, where would any of us've been but for Tom!

Where we are today, I dare say, up the ruddy pole granted you and Titch.

Ai, bloody awful business that, isn't it! Ought t'be scrapping these old machines now after this; prehistoric. Second man in a coupla weeks, in't it; these electric ones, now haven't I always told him Tom, the times we've been on to that, you know it don't you. Can't listen, old Titch, always been his trouble ha'n't it? Win every time.

Ai, bloody mess now all round. As you say.

That furnace door now. Been on to him ages ha'n't I, get that hinge fixed, ha'n't I Tom, you c'n swear to that yourself, can't you now?

Time and again, I know. Years now, in't it!

Who would've thought a hinge would do him in, a thing like that! Come away you know under his weight moment he braced on it. You know a thing like that gets stuck you've got to use your weight, just came crashing down onto the Oh God what a business eh? You been to see him I suppose?

Circulating today, know how it is; can't get up there till later can I? He's poorly though they say. How about them drawings you wanted, he give them to you?

Drawings?

You come in for Lho's old drawings this morning, didn't you?

Would you believe it slipped my mind completely, talking. You know the way he goes on, one thing to the next, slipped my mind completely. Saves up his thoughts, doesn't he, old Titch, hour after hour in that busy little skull, then catches you somewhere, anywhere, among the machines, any place so long's he can read your lips, then squanders them. On and on, Lamb's Margarine, Croat's Soaps, the lot. Running your blue today aren't you

126

– no not a word, never remembered a word about the drawings.

Got his reasons I daresay, copyright and that you know, the usual thing. None my business of course.

Dunno, maybe he'll never know, come to think of it, I mean never miss them once he's better, that's what I been thinking, Tom.

Poorly you know, in a coma they say, who knows! All bandaged up an' poorly.

Ai, who knows! Like you say. Never be the same around here again, that's for sure, in't it! Bet you'll be missing him messing around and that, always was a good soldier like, down to the job, no fooling, backbone of the old firm, old Titch, wasn't he!

Well he isn't dead yet, who knows, live in hope don't we. Marvellous these days they are with science o'course; might be hale and hearty as ever in a couple of weeks, what you might be calling right as rain once he gets over the worst, mightn't he?

Not much they can do about extensive burns like that Tom, no it isn't much they can do you'd be surprised. Depends if the brain is affected yes or no. Take these pilots in the war, racing drivers and that, it isn't much they can do with those kinds of burns at all, I been asking around, specially when infection sets in there's no telling.

Ai that's life, isn't it, here today gone tomorrow like; never know whose turn it'll be next as me mother always says. Day of reckoning and that, in't it.

Ai, except of course there's some as do their reckoning day by day, if you get my meaning; you picks your choice. Fellow in the van, young chap, he's dead?

Instantly. Going hell for leather round this curve you see, just asking for it wasn't he, traffic along here being what it is. Had it. Kaput. Finished. Just like that. Makes you think, dunnit!

It had a Conway trade name they say, poor chap. In the midst of life, ah well, got to be lived with hasn't it, the one sure thing as they say.

He's not dead yet of course, old Titch, but happen so he mightn't never…

Never what – say what you mean, why did you stop, mightn't never what Tom, what's y'meaning?

…never, you know, remember, I was thinking…

Remember?

You know how these things are, shock and that, it all happen so sudden like, didn't it? I expect it took even you aback a bit, must've done I wouldn't be surprised. Loss of memory, amnesia sort of, so he won't be remembering what really happened like, it won't be…

You'll be staying on here I suppose, I mean you would like that wouldn't you Tom? Not much else doing around here for chaps like you is there? What with your old ma and one thing and another you'd be wanting to stay on in the old firm wouldn't you then?

Never thought of leaving the old firm Joss, whatever give you such a queer idea? I mean it stands to reason I wouldn't be knowing where to turn as you say, it would finish the old girl off too before you could say Jack Rabbit…

Robinson, old man, Jack Robinson; that's what the saying is: drop of a hat, batting of an eye sort of thing. Yes, it would finish her off I suppose, leaving her cottage where she was born and that. Isn't easy.

It's what I been puzzling to meself all day long: Titch must've fallen being as he was, deaf and that and not hearing the kettle boiling as you might say, he would've fallen all by himself; in circumstances like that there's no saying is there, it's the only way I been thinking.

One thing you know: One must look always upon oneself in a reasonable light concerning things one has done or not done, or simply not yet done…

Yes Joss, sure…

…or which one might have no wish at all to do…

I don't think I'm getting your meaning there Joss, beg y'pardon.

Was a youngster fell from Trwyn Mawr bird's-nesting last summer, wasn't there?

You wrote the story yourself Joss, I remember yes.

Hard lines on the poor sod who run him over, wouldn't you say?

I see what you mean.

You couldn't say the poor kid *oughtn't* to have fallen, could you now? You couldn't say he oughtn't to've fallen in the other chap's way, could you? You couldn't even say the two had nothing to do with each other – you couldn't prove it.

That's a good one, that, I never thought of that before, good in't it! Now I'd better be handing you over them drawings, hadn't I?

Drawings?

Whatever you want, like. Anything you say Joss.

A *reasonable* light Tom, in every kind of situation. There's situations you see, like life's-breath, no man may order them, get that Tom?

Ai, you could say that I suppose, like me mother always says: The mind of this world it don't belong only to God, that's what me mother always says.

Wrong Tom, your ma's wrong. Everything in this whole wide world belongs to God like they say in Sunday School. It's what poor Lho found out, that's what did him in if you want to know. Just couldn't take it you see. He loved beauty and goodness and all that, the poor sod, it did him in. It's the reason he kept on and on about this Third Temptation and that. No fool, old Lho; he was no fool, Tom.

Ai, best designer west of the border you always used to say didn't you. Give a dog his due, don't you now!

And if God gives you a granite mountain to eat He sees to it that you eat it to the last pebble Tom, that's about the size of it so far's I can see, because listen: *No man can destroy God!* Equipped as he is a man may not do that. What's the tolling been for all day long do you suppose, gets on your nerves, don't it.

What tolling? Ain't been no tolling today Joss, I'd've heard wouldn't I, just under the bell tower as I am. You'll be popping down later I suppose, down the hospital I mean, what a business eh?

A reasonable light Tom, that's the real point, there isn't any other. *It's up to you!* Bid's waiting lunch now, I must dash. Sandra's flying home today, her card's a beauty, I nearly forgot.

Seems hardly time ago, don't it, since the wedding.

Och ai, time flies.

All the best to the young couple then, the best in life to them.

Lucky aren't you you old stick, everything you've ever asked haven't you? Rest on y'laurels now an' let the younger generation get on with it eh? 'Ere, y'never took them drawings, just a mo', won't take a minute, hang on will you?

No hurry, Tom, I'll be hanging on, no hurry.

As he eases another dense spill of the crowd across the zebra the eyes of the constable once again light on the figures of two men by the kerb, outside Masons the Shoe Shop, their backs silhouetted against the display piled to the ceiling of the show window. Their silhouettes do not reveal the colour of the pale blue anorak worn by the one nor the pattern of dog-tooth check in the jacket of the other.

The man with the brilliant false teeth has a lilac complexion. Price of progress, in't it! he is heard to remark, Can't have y'cake and eat it too, stands t'reason. But my attention riveted on the POLYPLEX poster once more scrutinises the golden treasury of the blonde girl figured there: billows of blown hair trembling across her face, her neck, square shoulders, the ceaseless lock plunging into an ivory valley between her breasts, pellets of nipples unsheathed, pink, pouting. Between her breasts, under the face of Jesus, his head is buried in the summery cotton frock so that to the girl uncomfortably postured beneath him his utterances could equally well be groans of ecstasy or of despair, she has no means of telling since still he does not show his face. Above the collar of the anorak she observes threadlike wrinkles across his neck. Threads of blood trickling down the forehead of Jesus stop short above the shuttered eyes, deepening the Man-of-Sorrows expression but she is careful to avoid His eyes which now, strangely, beyond the burnished cascade of her hair, Joss observes, or does he briefly imagine it, to be questioningly open above the nipples of her breasts. She wonders: Hadn't we better go into the little room now case anyone should come? We're not managing it too well this way, are we? But a vehicle at that moment decelerating for Parry Road might well have hit the kerb, a wall, a pillar or post for the explosion of shattered glass and stone which instantly brings the lovers to their feet, the woman clutching at the dishevelled clothing about her breasts. In which posture momentarily frozen as it were they realise – though their intimate play has come to so rude an end – that there has been no accident outside; there is only the shattered face of Jesus, the shuttered eyes, the broken picture cord, on the flagstones. She screams, a hollow quivering scream in the same instant as Joss gasps: The picture cord! Her frantic echo raps against the roof but Joss explains: Now, don't be so silly Love, once more encircling her buttocks. It's only a broken picture cord, you're not superstitious, are you? But on the flagstones the fragments of glass flash and glitter; the blonde girl flees, hair streaming, through the aisle door and bangs it shut, fumbling at her naked breasts.

Pivoting, the eyes of the constable light on the bronze figure of the Welsh Martyr rising you might say from an ocean of blood, its undiscriminating gaze fixed on the restless tides of Sweeley Street, a gaze whose objectivity the constable might well envy, persons and objects being so uniformly unemotive from this godlike view. For desirable as it might seem he may not escape the workings of cause and effect in the constricted visual field, the expanding and contracting aural frame of which he is the centre, a constriction of reference which appertains to no more than threescore yards or so, beyond which a body surrenders its identity and merges into the general ambience. And this colours the judgment, it might occur to him, with a relativity from which he cannot justly escape should he wish to be objective. Chance conversations, fragments of opinions, actions initiated beyond the visual field or the aural frame, haphazard observations which ascribe to this person, that thing, a significance which they do not inherently possess, facts unexplained. The man in the blue anorak for instance leaves the glass and oak door of The County in the company of a person with a lilac complexion who now appears to the constable for the first time so that asked he might insist with apparent truth: This person first appeared in the vicinity of the Pike Street roundabout at 11.50 a.m. or thereabouts, to which the constable might add that not once in two hours had he moved from his island. On the pavements the holiday crowd is about equally divided, the shadow side of Sweeley Street having now disappeared. Strolling on their shadows in the brilliant sunlight their movement condenses, expands, coagulates so to speak at migrant points between the Great Western and the rock, between the rock and the Great Western, people wearing less and less as the day progresses. Does it mean anything at all that now this man with the lilac complexion (who has just crossed the street) enters the paper shop into which the blonde girl carrying a plastic mac has already disappeared? What profit is to be drawn from observation of the fact other than just the noting of the fact itself? What anyway is to be made of the behaviour of this blonde girl who all the morning apparently, without purpose or direction, has drifted now here, now there over various stretches of Sweeley Street (for she is understandably among the very earliest of individuals noted by the constable on taking up his vigil on the island) always alone (he might swear) but with every indication, strangely now, of growing restlessness, uneasiness, or, it might even be thought, emotional stress? Or the evident agitation of the young man in a gaberdine mac dodging through the crowd from the direction of St John's frantically bellowing: Joss!

The two meet at the head of the zebra, outside Woolworths. Sean's look of death is more absolute than ever.

I've *been*, he declares, *everywhere*. Not a trace!

All the litter bins? Every last gutter and drain? The sewers? Sure? There's rubbish everywhere Sean, we live in the thick of decay it's easy to see, don't you go giving up so easily, me boy.

Joss you swine!

No end to the mess is there? Keep right on searching me lad, y'never can tell, love's not all that easy to find once lost, you can take my word on that.

Out comes the paperback novel from his pocket. Have a look at this Joss, I found it on the floor in there, by the picture – some lout's smashed that thing of Jesus by the way, now what!

The postcard is of *St Veronica's Handkerchief*: the violently coloured Christ, the conventional crown of thorns; threads of blood trickle to the shuttered eyes.

She'd like this one better I daresay, much better don't you think?

What's the tolling been for all day long, d'y'suppose?

I'll make a party, that's what I think I'll do Joss. Even if she won't come back I'll do that – make a hell'va party for her just the same. Christ, tell me, did that letter really say I'd do myself in?

It's all you *can* do you clot; shed your pain, man, father a legend, it's so easy, make her your murderer, it's what everybody else's doing, isn't it? There's only these two kinds of men me lad, them with whips, and them with wounds…

Thus spake Lho, I suppose?

No, thus spake Titch. Becoming another myth already you see, old Titch, a heritage – Get that situation Adonis? Now listen, that postcard belongs to *my* bitch old man, hand it over, quick.

Pivoting on his island the constable once more beckons the ends of the zebra. He realises that the group of motorcyclists just now beyond his visual field (the noise is already thunderous) will soon be upon him but his attention is for the moment caught by a young woman in a black trouser suit concluding a perilous crossing with a loaded pushchair. Guiltily she avoids the constable's eyes which are fixed now on a dense knot of bystanders at the head of the zebra on his left, between whose legs the figures of the two men, one in a gaberdine mac the other in a pale blue anorak, can be observed struggling on the kerb. Then the decelerating blast of youthful motorcyclists is upon him.

SNACKS.

These men were not drunk as some had supposed, even though one of them, the older, the one in the blue anorak, had earlier been observed to leave The County. It is thought that they parted friends.

12 noon.

The young girl at the head of the zebra bouncing a polka-dot beach ball in a nylon string bag against her knees looks at the constable leaving his island. Across the street she sees herself reflected in the show window of Cassels by the door of which (she notices it for the first time) a pillar-box stands on its purple shadow in the sun. There are four black bars in the zebra to the edge of the island, four white. She estimates that her normal step will not take her from bar to bar of the same colour so that in order to cross in this way she hops along the whites on the right leg to the island, there changes to the left and completes the crossing along the blacks to the kerb, smiling at her brilliant reflection in the stationers.

No. 5 size 10" x 8" matching envelopes No. 5 size white. Ref. 73091/66E. Made in Great Britain. Specially printed for Cassels, Stationers, 33 Sweeley Street, Caedmon, Est. 1898.

At the foot of the bronze statue the island now lies bare in the sun.

ABOUT THE AUTHOR

Denis Williams was born in Georgetown, Guyana, in 1923. As well as authoring two novels, Williams was a highly accomplished artist, who also taught and published in the fields of West Indian and African art and anthropology, and, from 1974, was Director of Art and Archaeology with Guyana's Ministry of Education and Culture. In addition to numerous prizes for his paintings, Williams was awarded the Golden Arrow of Achievement Award from the Government of Guyana in 1973. He died in 1998.

CARIBBEAN MODERN CLASSICS

2009/10 titles

Jan R. Carew
Black Midas
Introduction: Kwame Dawes
ISBN: 9781845230951; pp. 272; 23 May 2009; £9.99

This is the bawdy, Eldoradean epic of the legendary 'Ocean Shark' who makes and loses fortunes as a pork-knocker in the gold and diamond fields of Guyana, discovering that there are sharks with far sharper teeth in the city. *Black Midas* was first published in 1958.

Jan R. Carew
The Wild Coast
Introduction: Jeremy Poynting
ISBN: 9781845231101; pp. 240; 23 May 2009; £9.99

First published in 1958, this is the coming-of-age story of a sickly city child, sent away to the remote Berbice village of Tarlogie. Here he must find himself, make sense of Guyana's diverse cultural inheritances and come to terms with a wild nature disturbingly red in tooth and claw.

Neville Dawes
The Last Enchantment
Introduction: Kwame Dawes
ISBN: 9781845231170; pp. 332; 27 April 2009; £9.99

This penetrating and often satirical exploration of the search for self in a world divided by colour and class is set in the context of the radical hopes of Jamaican nationalist politics in the early 1950s. First published in 1960, the novel asks many pertinent questions about the Jamaica of today.

Wilson Harris
Heartland
Introduction: Michael Mitchell
ISBN: 9781845230968; pp. 104; 23 May 2009; £7.99

First published in 1964, this visionary narrative tracks one man's psychic disintegration in the aloneness of the forests of the Guyanese interior, making a powerful ecological statement about man's place in the 'invisible chain of being', in which nature is a no less active presence.

Edgar Mittelholzer
Corentyne Thunder
Introduction: Juanita Cox
ISBN: 9781845231118; pp. 242; 27 April 2009; £8.99

This pioneering work of West Indian fiction, first published in 1941, is not merely an acute portrayal of the rural Indo-Guyanese world, but a work of literary ambition that creates a symphonic relationship between its characters and the vast openness of the Corentyne coast.

Andrew Salkey
Escape to an Autumn Pavement
Introduction: Thomas Glave
ISBN: 9781845230982; pp. 220; 23 May 2009; £8.99

This brave and remarkable novel, set in London at the end of the 1950s, and published in 1960, catches its 'brown' Jamaican narrator on the cusp between black and white, between exiled Jamaican and an incipient black Londoner, and between heterosexual and homosexual desires.

Denis Williams
Other Leopards
Introduction: Victor Ramraj
ISBN: 9781845230678; pp. 216; 23 May 2009; £8.99

Lionel Froad is a Guyanese working on an archeological survey in the mythical Jokhara in the horn of Africa. There he hopes to rediscover the self he calls 'Lobo', his alter ego from 'ancestral times', which he thinks slumbers behind his cultivated mask. First published in 1963, this is one of the most important Caribbean novels of the past fifty years.

Denis Williams
The Third Temptation
Introduction: Victor Ramraj
ISBN: 9781845231163; pp. 140; May 2010; £7.99

A young man is killed in a traffic accident at a Welsh seaside resort. Around this incident, Williams, drawing inspiration from the *Nouveau Roman*, creates a reality that is both rich and problematic. Whilst he brings to the novel a Caribbean eye, Williams makes an important statement about refusing any restrictive boundaries for Caribbean fiction. The novel was first published in 1968.

Roger Mais
The Hills Were Joyful Together
Introduction: Norval Edwards
ISBN: 9781845231002; pp. 272; August 2010; £9.99

Unflinchingly realistic in its portrayal of the wretched lives of Kingston's urban poor, this is a novel of prophetic rage. First published in 1953, it is both a work of tragic vision and a major contribution to the evolution of an autonomous Caribbean literary aesthetic.

Edgar Mittelholzer
A Morning at the Office
Introduction: Raymond Ramcharitar
ISBN: 978184523; pp. 208; May 2010; £8.99

First published in 1950, this is one of the Caribbean's foundational novels in its bold attempt to portray a whole society in miniature. A genial satire on human follies and the pretensions of colour and class, this novel brings several ingenious touches to its mode of narration.

Edgar Mittelholzer
Shadows Move Among Them
Introduction: tba
ISBN: 9781845230913; pp. 352; May 2010; £10.99

In part a satire on the Eldoradean dream, in part an exploration of the possibilities of escape from the discontents of civilisation, Mittelholzer's 1951 novel of the Reverend Harmston's attempt to set up a utopian commune dedicated to 'Hard work, frank love and wholesome play' has some eerie 'pre-echoes' of the fate of Jonestown in 1979.

Edgar Mittelholzer
The Life and Death of Sylvia
Introduction: Juanita Cox
ISBN: 9781845231200; pp. 362; May 2010, £10.99

In 1930s' Georgetown, a young woman on her own is vulnerable prey, and when Sylvia Russell finds she cannot square her struggle for economic survival and her integrity, she hurtles towards a wilfully early death. Mittelholzer's novel of 1953 is a richly inward portrayal of a woman who finds inner salvation through the act of writing.

Elma Napier
A Flying Fish Whispered
Introduction: Evelyn O'Callaghan
ISBN: 9781845231026; pp. 248; July 2010; £8.99

With one of the most delightfully feisty women characters in Caribbean
fiction and prose that sings, Elma Napier's 1938 Dominican novel is a
major rediscovery, not least for its imaginative exploration of different
kinds of Caribbeans, in particular the polarity between plot and plan-
tation that Napier sees in a distinctly gendered way.

Orlando Patterson
The Children of Sisyphus
Introduction: Kwame Dawes
ISBN: 9781845230944; pp. 288; August 2010; £9.99

This is a brutally poetic book that brings to the characters who live on
Kingston's 'dungle' an intensity that invests them with tragic depth. In
Patterson's existentialist novel, first published in 1964, dignity comes
with a stoic awareness of the absurdity of life and the shedding of false
illusions, whether of salvation or of a mythical African return.

V.S. Reid
New Day
Introduction: Norval Edwards
ISBN: 9781845230906, pp. 360; August 2010, £9.99

First published in 1949, this historical novel focuses on defining
moments of Jamaica's nationhood, from the Morant Bay rebellion of
1865, to the dawn of self-government in 1944. *New Day* pioneers the
creation of a distinctively Jamaican literary language of narration.

Garth St. Omer
A Room on the Hill
Introduction: John Robert Lee
ISBN: 9781845230937; pp. 210; September 2010; £8.99

A friend's suicide and his profound alienation in a St Lucia still
slumbering in colonial mimicry and the straitjacket of a reactionary
Catholic church drive John Lestrade into a state of internal exile. First
published in 1968, St. Omer's meticulously crafted novel is a pioneering exploration of the inner Caribbean man.

Wayne Brown, *On the Coast*
George Campbell, *First Poems*
Austin C. Clarke, *The Survivors of the Crossing*
Austin C. Clarke, *Amongst Thistles and Thorns*
O.R. Dathorne, *The Scholar Man*
O.R. Dathorne, *Dumplings in the Soup*
Neville Dawes, *Interim*
Wilson Harris, *The Eye of the Scarecrow*
Wilson Harris, *The Sleepers of Roraima*
Wilson Harris, *Tumatumari*
Wilson Harris, *Ascent to Omai*
Wilson Harris, *The Age of the Rainmakers*
Marion Patrick Jones, *Panbeat*
Marion Patrick Jones, *Jouvert Morning*
Earl Lovelace, *Whilst Gods Are Falling*
Roger Mais, *Black Lightning*
Una Marson, *Selected Poems*
Edgar Mittelholzer, *Children of Kaywana*
Edgar Mittelholzer, *The Harrowing of Hubertus*
Edgar Mittelholzer, *Kaywana Blood*
Edgar Mittelholzer, *My Bones and My Flute*
Edgar Mittelholzer, *A Swarthy Boy*
Orlando Patterson, *An Absence of Ruins*
V.S. Reid, *The Leopard* (North America only)
Garth St. Omer, *Shades of Grey*
Andrew Salkey, *The Late Emancipation of Jerry Stover*
and more…